'One of the most unsettling an ....erican writers today. (…) Trías is insatiable and a great storyteller.'
El Cultural

'An extraordinary novel.'
Giuseppe Caputo

'An intense and dark novel with luminous writing: I admit to being dazzled.'
Liliana Heker

'Fernanda Trías has crafted a unique world that we feel ineluctably drawn to.'
La Vanguardia

'Trías narrates what seems to be impossible to narrate: the seeds of pain, the trembling feat that is the attachment to life.'
Giovanna Rivero

'Fernanda Trías cuts her phrases with a scalpel to get to the very marrow of language.'
La voz de Galicia

'Family, intimacy, and madness intertwine in this exceptional story by Trías.'
Revista Ñ

'Many read *The Rooftop* like a disturbing love story between a daughter and her father, but it is much more than that. It's the genesis of everything that Trías would move on to write.'
WMagazín

THE ROOFTOP

First published by Charco Press 2021
Charco Press Ltd., Office 59, 44-46 Morningside Road,
Edinburgh EH10 4BF

This book was published with funding from the IDA Programme from Uruguay
XXI and the Ministry of Education & Culture of Uruguay / Este libro fue
publicado gracias al Programa IDA de Uruguay XXI y el MEC.

A CIP catalogue record for this book is available from the British Library.

ISBN: 9781913867041
e-book: 9781913867058

www.charcopress.com

Edited by Fionn Petch
Cover designed by Pablo Font
Typeset by Laura Jones
Proofread by Fiona Mackintosh

2 4 6 8 10 9 7 5 3 1

Fernanda Trías

THE ROOFTOP

Translated by
Annie McDermott

CHARCO PRESS

If they came right now they'd find me face-up on the bed, in the same position I collapsed down in around midnight. Eleven thirty-eight, to be precise: the time when I last looked at the clock and the time when everything ended. I gave Flor a kiss, told her to sleep tight, and she closed her eyes like it was just another night.

The candle guttered out a while ago, and now the darkness is swallowing the walls. It's almost as if the whole world knew and was lying in wait just for me. I'm not sure what time it is, but the later it gets the less frightened I feel, and the less I feel of anything at all. Whatever happens, they'll have to break down the door, because I put the chain on and wedged the chest of drawers against it. Dad and Flor are in the other room and in a funny way they're keeping each other company. Not me. I don't have anyone, but I'm determined to stay awake.

I hear a siren in the distance: an ambulance or a police car, I can never tell which. As it draws closer, my heart pounds in my chest. The sound turns shrill and leaves me shellshocked as it goes by under the window. Red light flashed onto the walls for a moment, like tiny flame-figures dancing in the air. Now the siren fades as well, and I'm back in the shadowy silence of the room. Alone. I have to convince myself that what's in the other room isn't a man, isn't Dad. Tucked up together it was like they were sleeping.

It's hard to believe I had a life before this one, a job, a flat, which I now remember nothing about. For me, real life began with Julia's death, went on for four years and came to an end today.

The bird smell had taken over Dad's bedroom. Some days I opened the window to air it out, but the air had got used to staying put, like a whirlwind stuck in purgatory. When I mentioned this, he said it was my fault, for keeping the window closed for months on end.

'Well, whenever I opened it you'd start screaming for help like a maniac. Three times I saved you from getting carted off to the loony bin.'

That was in the beginning, the days when he yelled at me every time I went in with his food. Once he even faked a choking fit. His face swelled up from coughing so much and he flailed his arms like a giant dragonfly. Gradually, with time, he gave up on yelling. Maybe he learned to love me a little; or maybe it was because of Flor, though he took a while to come round to all that.

I read a long time ago that a twelve-week-old foetus is the same size as an orange. The photo in the book showed a black rectangle with a fuzzy white half-moon floating in the middle. If I turned the page sideways, it looked like a smile or a winking eye. Those months and the ones leading up to them, when Dad was calm and didn't shout, were a happy time. The baby would move and even speak, with a purring sound only I could hear. Back then I had a wild hope that lasted until after Flor was born. Then it began to fall away, and I didn't even notice.

I was patient with Dad. I wanted him to touch my belly and listen to the soft burbling noises coming from inside me, but I waited a bit longer before asking him. One day I made up my mind and went into his room. It was an unusual time, mid-afternoon, and Dad stared when he saw me empty-handed. He was lying on his right side, on top of the blankets, with one elbow on the pillow. I went over and lifted up my sweater.

'See how it's grown,' I said, showing him my belly. 'Sixteen weeks.'

He didn't even look. He closed his eyes, turned over in bed and lay motionless with his face to the wall. I don't know why he got into those moods. One day he'd be fine and make room for me on the bed, and the next he wouldn't even speak to me. It had got worse after I told him about the baby, that soon we were going to have one just for us.

'We'll be a family again,' I said, but he didn't take it well and pouted like a petulant child.

Dad could be like that when he wanted to be, sulky and more stubborn than anyone.

I suppose the flat didn't help. The bedroom never got any direct light, just a faint glimmer when the sun shone hard on the big church wall opposite. On those days, the bird sang more than ever. Dad would sit up slightly in bed, facing the cage, and toss birdseed at it like old men do in town squares. The same weary, blank expression: the stiff body and a single arm moving by itself.

The church wall, that grey ocean wave that blocks the view from both windows, has always blighted our life. Dad wouldn't tell me if the church was built before or after Julia bought the flat. I was four when we moved here and all I remember is the bustle of removal men carrying furniture up the stairs. Amid the chaos of dust and boxes, I wandered in circles like a little blind hen, colliding with the workers' hairy legs. I searched the forest of limbs for Dad's, but I couldn't tell which they were. That's all I remember. The rest I forgot or never took in. As for the wall, nothing.

Carmen says Julia could have bought a flat near the beach.

'She was a fool not to,' she told me one day.

I think Julia felt protected by the shadow of the wall. She never went to mass on Sundays; she preferred having the church to herself and used to go over during the siesta, when most people forget about saints. She sat in the pews at the back and gazed at the air; I suppose she was hoping something special would happen. It was physical proximity that mattered to her: getting as close as she could to God's back. Maybe she thought she was safe from harm next to that big church wall. But she was wrong. Sometimes I went with Julia to church. I crawled around under the pews until my tights were grubby and laddered at the knees. I liked the smell of the fresh varnish, especially if I could pick off the hard little beads and suck on them like sweets. Julia prayed or stared straight ahead. The air is so strange inside churches. Sticky and thick with presences.

I don't know when everything started to go wrong, or what set the end in motion. At one point I thought it was the pregnancy. Now, with nothing left to do but look back, I don't think there was ever a beginning, just one long ending that devoured us bit by bit. If I'm remembering all this tonight, it's only because I want a little more time with them. No one could possibly understand how I feel: isolated, expecting nothing, knowing I'm locked in a desperate battle to defend something that's already gone.

Five or six months pregnant, no more: I was in the kitchen cooking meat for myself and carrot purée for Dad, who only ever ate vegetables. Just that morning I'd told him he was going to turn into a canary if he carried on like that, and fly away through the window. I was laughing when I said it. He didn't answer, but his eyes gleamed as if he were imagining something.

'Don't even think about it,' I said.

Sometimes I was afraid he really would turn into a bird. On those days I closed the shutters, and I even used to have nightmares. I'd see him sprout feathers, first behind his ears, like tufts of grey hair, then under his arms and over the rest of his body. I always woke up before the transformation was complete.

I opened the bedroom door, balancing the tray in one hand, and switched on the light. It was winter, June or July, I don't know, but you needed the lights on even in the daytime. He was lying all bunched up like a used handkerchief, awake and open-eyed, and he didn't even say hello. I put the tray by the bed and sat down next to him.

'I brought you some carrot. Didn't you say you wanted carrot?'

No response. His eyes closed, or he closed them. He said he was thinking about the seafront, about the walls running along it and the waves crashing against the pier, like when he used to go fishing.

'Why think about that,' I replied. 'The walls are covered in rust and the water smells rotten. People who fish there get poisoned and die,' I said.

5

The bird had made a mess in the cage and gone to sleep standing up, its head tucked into its chest.

'It's shat itself again,' I said.

'It's a bird. It doesn't shit itself. It shits.'

'Either way, I'm the one who has to deal with it. I do everything around here, and no one else lifts a finger.'

I removed the newspaper from the floor of the cage and checked there was water in the dish. Then I heard my father's voice, energetic now, saying he wanted to go out, that I should let him go to the seafront.

'Dad, please. What's got that into your head again?'

I tried to seem calm but my back stiffened and I felt a twinge in my neck, as if a knot of thoughts and words had formed there. I'd have liked to tell Dad that the world was going under, that we were the only possible world, and that, besides, if he went he would end up hating it.

But something else came out instead, uncontrollable and dripping with rage:

'There's no sea, no square, no church, no nothing. The world is what's under this roof.'

Dad groaned, as if he were straining to cry, and said he wouldn't see another human as long as he lived.

He was so pathetic when he cried, like a bratty little kid. I even found myself wanting to hurt him, because after all, he was the one who taught me that you have to be strong in this life, and that tears and emotional outbursts get you nowhere. I didn't enjoy feeling like that, afraid of what I might do. It was the same when I was younger, when Julia used to tell me not to tread on the flowers in the square. *Keep off the grass*, the sign said, but the moment Julia looked away I'd go tearing across the flowerbed in a frantic dash, glancing back at her over my shoulder as my feet sank into the freshly dug earth. Then I'd step out of the flowerbed and carefully clean off the soil, wiping the soles of my shoes on the grass. Most of the time, I couldn't bring myself to look at the trail of trampled flowers in my wake. I was scared someone would tell me off or even call the police. One afternoon, when we got home, Julia asked why my socks were so muddy. I immediately burst into tears. I was shaking and my face was smeared with snot.

'What's wrong with her?' asked Dad.

'I've had it up to here with her, that's what.'

'You're not my mum,' I sobbed.

Dad gave me a hug and led me out to the balcony.

'That's right, take her side!' Julia yelled at him.

The truth is, I liked those flowers, and I don't know why it was so tempting to tread on them. I always felt guilty afterwards and imagined them growing back, stronger and more beautiful than before.

The argument with Dad was left unresolved. He'd tried so hard to cry that now he'd set himself off in earnest. I told him to be quiet, that behaving like that wouldn't fix anything, but he buried his head in the pillow and told me to leave him alone.

I went to the kitchen to get the water bottle. For some reason I couldn't stop thinking about rabbits; I'd always wanted to have a white one and call it Popi. I used to have a box hidden under my bed where I was planning to keep it, because Dad promised to buy me one every time he fought with Julia. But in the end it never happened. Julia didn't like them because they left little poos like chocolate-covered peanuts everywhere, ate the houseplants and carried disease.

Back in Dad's room, I poured him some water and put the glass on a napkin on the bedside table. He'd stopped crying. His fists were clenched and the skin on his knuckles was white and stretched. I took hold of his hand and the fingers slowly uncurled and went limp.

'Just a few more months till the baby comes,' I said. 'It's a boy, I can tell. Isn't that what you've always wanted? Look.'

I unbuttoned my blouse so he could see how my breasts were growing. They were hard, with blue veins. He looked at them, curious, but then it was as if he'd suddenly remembered something horrible and his face changed.

'Do that up,' he said. 'I don't want anything. I want to be alone.'

That evening he still wouldn't touch the tray of food, and when I went in to change the canary's water there were vegetables all over the parquet floor. Some were squashed flat, and it was impossible to dig out the scraps from between the boards. As I swept and scrubbed, he stayed under the covers, which were pulled up right over his head. My throat was like sandpaper, but I held back from saying anything that might make things worse. It was getting harder and harder to crouch down to clean; my belly was heavy and at night I could never find a comfortable position, which meant I was always tired.

'Do you want the tablets?' I asked.

He didn't answer. We both knew he couldn't sleep without them, but he was in such a sulk that he'd have stayed awake all night sooner than speak to me.

'In that case I'll have to lock the window…'

From among the pillows, I heard the whistle of his lungs and the slurp of his blocked nose.

'Leave them there,' he said at last.

I put them on the bedside table next to the water glass and turned off the lamp.

'See you tomorrow,' I said. 'Sweet dreams.'

I went over and kissed his hand, the only part of his body not under the covers, but it didn't even twitch.

I'd long given up on wearing trousers. Lycra ones were so tight I felt stifled. Jeans and other fabrics simply didn't do up. Sometimes I imagined the baby struggling inside me, pushing with its hands and feet to make my flesh give way like elastic. I was scared Dad would find me ugly and never want to touch me again. Julia had been slim and athletic, and Dad used to tell her it made him proud to have a wife like that.

That night I dreamt I got so fat I turned into a whale and some sailors hoisted me up by the tail and flung me into the sea. Dad was one of the sailors. He was laughing and splashing around on the shore. I woke up feeling panicked, my heart pounding, and ran into his room. It was five a.m. He and the bird were both asleep, with their chins tucked into their chests. The shutters were bolted shut.

Later, around seven, Dad started calling my name. The sun was just beginning to rise and a faint light seeped in around the edges of the window.

'What is it? Are you okay?'

He couldn't breathe, or was pretending he couldn't. He begged me to open the window, saying he and the canary were suffocating. 'We're suffocating,' were his exact words. Whenever he talked about himself and the bird he said 'we'.

'I can't open the window. Haven't you noticed it's the middle of winter? Do you want to make yourself ill?'

He pointed at the canary. I went over to the cage and practically stuck my nose through the bars.

'Turn the light on,' he said.

I switched on the lamp, tricking the bird, which woke up and shook out its feathers.

'See? It's alive.'

That afternoon, Carmen dropped off the shopping I'd asked for. When I opened the door, she pushed the bags through with her foot, then came inside and flopped down in the armchair in the living room. She cupped her hands around her nose, which was pink from the cold, and blew into them. Into her huge, hairy hands. The plastic bags had left white furrows on her skin. I took everything into the kitchen and, before she could say anything, put the water on for the herbal infusion she'd recommended me.

From the kitchen I could hear Carmen huffing and puffing, grumbling about the weather and how expensive everything was. A few times she asked me how I was feeling, but she didn't let me respond. Instead, she launched straight back into her complaints about the winter, the cold and the dangers of catching the flu at her time of life. What with her foreign accent and the whistling kettle, I could barely make out what she was saying.

I returned with the two mugs and we sat at the table. When I put my lips to the ceramic rim, the bitter smell of the leaves pricked my nostrils.

'It's good for you,' she said when she saw me grimace. 'Drrink up.'

I sniffed again and took a small sip. The shards of unstrained leaf scratched my throat.

'So, how's yourr fatherr doing?'

'Not good. Really ill. He's delirious again.'

Carmen sighed and rolled her eyes.

'Such a shame, dearr. So vorrying for you. And vhat about that man who comes over sometimes – is he your boyfriend?'

'Which man?'

'You know, the one vith the briefcase.'

'He's the medicine man.'

'And I bet that's not all he is,' she said, winking at me and giggling.

But I didn't laugh. She'd started nibbling the skin around her fingernails, a habit of hers, and I realised she was nervous.

'There's two of us in this flat and a third on the way,' I said. 'And that's all.'

'I underrstand, dear. I von't say a vorrd.'

Then she tried to change the subject, telling me about the baby she'd delivered the night before.

'The mother veighed twenty-two stone,' she said, as she fiddled with the teaspoon in her mug. 'She'd been flat on her back forr six months and I had to stick my arrm in rrright up to my elbow to pull the kid out. It looked like a pig, the poor thing. One of the thrree little pigs, I'm telling you.'

On the afternoons when Carmen came by with the herbal remedies, she interspersed stories of women giving birth with anecdotes from her childhood in some European country. Once she told me her father had been a very learned man who studied philosophy by a log stove. Carmen would sit on the floor with her two brothers and listen to her father's explanations. One day he told them about the energy of thought. He explained that thoughts were a kind of matter, meaning that we can make things happen simply by wanting them to; we just have to channel the energy right. One day a bomb fell on Carmen's house and killed her father and two brothers. Carmen saw them screaming

11

in the flames, but nobody could save them. She and her mother survived for several days by cooking mice on piles of burning books, before boarding the ship that brought them to these shores.

According to Carmen, it was possible to bring things about through thought alone. You had to sit somewhere comfortable, close your eyes and imagine what you wanted to achieve as if it had already happened. From the very moment you imagined it, she explained, the desire began to be fulfilled.

Ever since that day, I thought a lot about Julia. I'd stand and stare out of the kitchen window at the web of clotheslines criss-crossing the courtyard like veins inside a hollow body. And there, floating among the multicoloured twine, I'd see Julia's face, smiling the way I remembered it. I thought about her a lot, and about each of the times I'd hated her. And most of all I thought about how I might have caused the accident.

The wardrobe in my room is still full of Julia's stuff. I never got round to taking it all out or looking through the shoeboxes stacked on top. Aside from the photos and a handful of dresses, I couldn't bring myself to touch her things.

The dress I wore the most was a red polka-dot sundress, Dad's favourite. True, he never said a word, as if he didn't even recognise it, but every time I unlocked his door and slid half my leg through the gap, he started laughing uncontrollably. I swung my leg to and fro like a cabaret dancer and then gradually followed with an arm, a shoulder and the other leg, until my whole body was inside the room. That was the end of the game. Dad loved it when my leg first appeared through the gap, and I, with my ear pressed to the other side of the door, never tired of hearing his loud, abrupt quack of a laugh.

One day I woke him up dressed entirely as Julia, holding a cup of coffee. I sat on the bed and watched him. He looked so lovely, with his huge blue eyes and eyelashes that curled back all the way to his eyelids. He was still half-asleep, but he reached out an arm from under the covers and stroked my leg, ever so slowly, from top to bottom, his fingers skimming the soft fabric of the dress. I felt self-conscious and closed my eyes, but I opened them slightly a few times to peek under the lids; my eyelashes formed a kind of net, and no one would have known I was looking. His chest was jumping like a toad's and I silently prayed his hand would carry on going. Higher, just a little higher, in between my thighs. The dress had ridden up and he was stroking my leg with his warm, firm hand, feeling his way like a blind man. Then he came to the dress and gripped it tight; I thought he was going to tear it, but no, he let go and made space for me against the wall.

There are things I'd rather not think about. Sometimes even thought is a kind of invasion, like seeing yourself naked in the mirror: it's more embarrassing than if someone else were looking. I wonder if it wasn't those few encounters – red cat's eyes on a darkened road – that shaped the course of my life.

Then the dress lost its colour. I put something else red in the wash with it and the polka-dots went pink. Dad changed as well. My leg no longer made him laugh, and sometimes he even sobbed and murmured *Juli, Juli*, like in a nightmare.

Julia's room is exactly as it was before she died: the same tatty lace bedspread, the rocking chair, the bags in the wardrobe. The slippers are still under the bed and they look like two taxidermy cats. I think I was hoping they'd disintegrate by themselves, that they'd die like Julia died and stop tormenting me. But I never went near them. Even today, when they're finally going to be defiled by strangers, I couldn't bring myself to touch them.

All along I felt sure that, sooner or later, Dad would accept how much we wanted this baby. Now and then I still tried to make him touch my belly, but he was more obstinate than ever and wouldn't budge an inch.

'Two more months and everything will change,' I used to tell him. 'You'll see.'

He'd shake his head, turn his back on me and sometimes even yell:

'Shut up, Clara! Don't say that.'

'Haven't you always wanted a boy?'

'No, it's not possible. Get away from me, you liar.'

'Keep your voice down. Or do you want the whole building to find out?'

But by then he wasn't strong enough to shout the way he used to. Now shouting just meant waving his arms and turning red and ending up with a coughing fit. Then he'd ask for the sleeping tablets unprompted.

During those months, he kept on pestering me about the pier:

'I'll come back, I promise. Why don't we go together, have a bit of an outing?'

I asked him if he'd lost his mind, if he honestly thought I could go strolling along a cold, windy, polluted seafront in the middle of August in my condition.

'Just because you feel like it! Is there nothing you're not capable of?'

'There's nothing I am capable of,' he said, and covered his head with the pillow.

I felt dizzy, saw the flash of light that comes before blacking out, and had to lie on the floor with my legs raised. Carmen had taught me this technique and it really worked.

'It's our baby,' I said, when I could finally get up. 'That's all that counts.'

He didn't answer, but as I was leaving, when I was almost at the door, I heard him whisper:

'Liar.'

That afternoon I'd arranged to visit Carmen and go through the preparation exercises. It was the first time I'd been inside her flat and the place was horrendous. Rusty pots and pans, wooden spoons and bizarre ornaments hung from the walls. There was even a plastic palm tree in one corner of the bedroom.

She made me lie on the bed, on a fluffy blanket, and move my hips in circles. She shouted instructions from the foot of the bed and the palm leaves sprouted up behind her, giving her a shock of green hair.

'Up. Down. Up. Down.'

I didn't like those exercises; they made me feel ridiculous, like a dog writhing in the grass, but Carmen maintained they were essential and made them a condition of her being my midwife.

'Those are the rrrules,' she said. 'Vithout rrrules, the deal's off.'

I agreed to the exercises and the herbal remedies because I didn't want to go to hospital. Doctors ask too many questions, like the police, and they love turning up at people's houses and sniffing around their private business.

The last time I'd called a doctor was no exception. It had been two months since Julia died and I was worried about Dad. He wasn't eating, he couldn't sleep, he seemed delirious. So I called a doctor, but as soon as I hung up I knew I'd made a mistake. The doctor turned out to be a woman, and that made me uneasy. I watched as she examined him and asked him questions. He was in a bad mood and asked her how long it would be before he snuffed it.

'Don't be silly,' said the doctor. 'You've got a long life ahead of you, you can't give up now.'

On her way out, she took me aside. I'd been about to close the door, but she seemed to be holding it open with her foot. I thought she was going to push me and throw me out of my own home, because that's the sort of thing these people do, but no, she was in a hurry, and I suppose it wasn't the right time.

'He's still young,' she said. 'He needs a fresh start, that's all. If he's no better in a couple of months, I'd suggest seeing a psychiatrist.'

A *psychiatrist*, she said, as if we were mad.

'Don't stop, dearr,' Carmen shouted. 'Keep going, come on: up, down, up, down.'

My clothes felt too tight and I undid a few buttons as I went on thrusting my hips, inhaling and exhaling the way Carmen told me.

'Enough,' I said, and slumped down on the bed. I was dripping with sweat, and my belly felt heavier than a sack full of rocks.

Carmen cackled like a monkey and sat down beside me. I stared at her yellow, far-apart teeth. She reached out to touch me, but something made her stop and she tucked her hand between her legs.

'It's rrreally grrowing,' she said. 'October or November, no laterr than that.'

One Sunday in October I decided to go to the market; I wanted to get Dad a present, since he was still restless and sulking about the pier. It was a sunny day but the air was cool, almost cold for that time of year, and I put on a woolly hat. I held my belly as I walked, afraid someone would elbow me on their way past and hurt the baby. I planned my every move, anticipating the points of contact with the people walking towards me, and more than once I had to step off the pavement into the road. People are brutes: they push you, they tread on your feet, they don't watch where they're going with their shopping trolleys. Their eyes roam over your body, always maliciously. Before, when Dad and Julia lived alone and I was renting the flat on Magallanes, I liked going early to the Sunday market. Then came the accident and I moved in with Dad, and little by little I let go of everything that tied me to my previous life.

At weekends, Carmen went off to the Tent with the rest of her sect and she couldn't do my shopping. Everyone at the Tent spoke the same language as her and discussed natural remedies and the medicinal properties of plants. They also gave each other 'encouragement in life's daily battles' and supported each other 'like family'. That's what she told me, and I had no desire to ask anything else. I never found out where the Tent was or why it was called that. And I don't know what good finding out would have done; there were so many of them, after all, and only three of us.

What I wanted to buy that Sunday was a big fish tank, and some seaweed and colourful fish. I bought one from the first fish stall I came to, although the seller was very unpleasant and made a stupid joke about my woolly hat. 'So your thoughts don't freeze,' I think he said. He gave me the empty fish tank with some gravel at the bottom and the fish and seaweed in a plastic bag. There were two fish: an orange one with dead, staring eyes, and a blue and white one that dragged its tail behind it like a bridal train.

Before leaving I stopped to look at the rabbit cages. I poked my finger through the bars and into the soft white fur until I felt the creature's flank. I wanted to take one home with me, but I didn't in the end. If only I had, I think now, if only I'd done so many other things. The seller glared at me fiercely and pointed to the sign on one of the cages: *No touching the animals.* He looked at my hat as well, but fortunately he didn't say anything. I extracted my finger and walked quickly towards Avenida 18 de Julio.

When I reached the building entrance, I had a sore back and swollen arms from carrying the fish tank. I went up the first flight of steps thinking about Carmen; I imagined her in the Tent, depilating the backs of her hands and laughing at me as I carted the fish tank up the stairs, pausing for a few seconds on each landing.

I arrived home out of breath. The flat was warm and quiet, and Dad's bedroom door was closed. I filled the tank with water and dropped in the fish and the seaweed. It was too big for just two fish, but I thought I could add other things as time went on, such as one of those little castles that blow bubbles. It wasn't easy to lift the fish tank and put it on a chair; filled with water it was very heavy. I dragged the chair on two legs, pulling it by the backrest, and as I approached Dad's bedroom door I heard the canary cheeping. I thought the light must be on. Leaving the fish tank outside, hidden from view, I opened the door. Dad gave a start.

'Did you go out?' he asked. 'I was calling you. What was all that noise?'

The padlock was still on but there was a hole in one shutter, letting in a beam of light that made the scene look like a religious painting. The dust in the air was visible in the pale strip that landed on the cage.

'What have you done?' I asked. 'Are you out of your mind?'

I waited for an explanation, but he just shrugged and went on tossing birdseed into the cage, his features flat, like stones set in his face. There was a piece of splintered wood on the floor, and a knife.

'The wood was rotten,' he said.

I picked up the knife and brandished the handle at his temple, but I was so livid I didn't know what to say. He looked at me and shrugged again.

'It needs light, Clara. It's a bird, not a bat.'

I spent the rest of the morning watching the fish, especially the blue one as it swam to and fro, sweeping the water with its tail. I'd brought the fish tank into my bedroom. A rainbow had formed among the seaweed and it was as if the fish were swimming under a multicoloured bridge.

I didn't go back to Dad's room until lunchtime. I didn't feel like seeing him, so I went in and put the tray on the bedside table without saying a word. As I was leaving, he called me.

'Clara, come here.'

His blue eyes sought me out, shining. I went to the foot of the bed and he shifted closer to the edge.

'What do you want?'

'Come on. Don't be annoyed.'

I lay down next to the wall, like the other times, but I felt clumsy and gross; I couldn't relax. My hair was tied back, not loose and perfumed the way he liked it. I hadn't showered since the previous morning, either, which made me all too aware of the smells of my body. Dad slid one arm under my neck and with his other hand he pushed my head onto his chest. The damp warmth of his palm spread through my ear and I thought I heard the sound of crashing waves, as if his cupped hand were a seashell. As if his whole body were one of those gigantic shells that wash up on the shore.

I let my neck go floppy and listened to his heart. His chest inflated and deflated, and I thought my head might go rolling away like a coin. After a while he tried to say something, paused and then fell silent again. I was slowly melting in the heat of his bearlike skin, and all I wanted was for that moment never to end.

'Clara…' Don't spoil it, I thought, but I didn't have time to say anything. 'Just looking at the water, touching it. Where's the harm in that?'

His breathing had quickened. I thought about the fish tank, the colourful fish, and how happy he'd be when he saw them.

'Don't worry,' I said. 'Tomorrow morning you'll get a surprise.'

His body seemed stronger, stiller, and the embrace tightened.

'Only a month to go now. Carmen says November at the latest.'

'It'll do you good to get out as well, breathe some spring air.'

'Yes. And the water, the fish… Remember how you used to love going fishing?'

'Yes,' he said, and I think he smiled.

It was a while since I'd last opened Julia's wardrobe. As a girl I wondered what she could possibly keep in a wardrobe so enormous, as if it were a trunk full of mystery objects. I don't know why I expected anything other than clothes and shoes.

'Hands off, young lady,' she always said.

I used to watch her, secretly. Once I saw her open the top drawer and take out a seed germinator – some cotton wool and a few dry, withered beansprouts in the lid of a jar. Who keeps a seed germinator in their wardrobe? Julia, that's who. Meaning she could have had thousands of other things in there as well, and what's more I had to behave myself, or else she'd bring out the girl who lived inside the wardrobe and give her all my toys. My toys and my bed. And my food.

'Be good or I'll give it to my other little girl,' she always said.

The girl in the wardrobe could come out at any moment and take everything away from me.

Now I was looking for a nice dress. I hadn't seen Dad so excited in months, and I wanted the fish tank to be a special moment. I tried on several, though some were too old or too dated. I rummaged around, pulling out the hangers and throwing them on the bed, until I finally found one I liked. It looked slightly ridiculous because my belly made it shorter in front than behind, but it had a pretty embroidered neckline. Julia spent a fortune on clothes, and Dad never said anything. It was her money, after all.

Among the dresses, at the back of the wardrobe, I found a box of newspaper cuttings, letters and photos.

As I looked through them I couldn't shake the feeling that Julia was waiting outside the door, ready to yell at me for touching her stuff. The feeling was so strong that I had to get up and inspect the whole flat to make sure she wasn't there. On returning to her room, I locked the door and couldn't help but laugh at myself. Although I was laughing at Julia as well, because she was never coming back.

The cuttings were so old I could barely read them. They were from before the year when Julia and Dad got married, articles in which Julia was named Miss Springtime and photographed holding a trophy. I examined her closely and thought she looked fat. How could she have been Miss Springtime? I screwed that cutting up and threw it away. Then I put the letters back in the box and didn't even check who'd written them.

The photos kept me entertained for a while. Some showed a young, smiling Julia hugging people I didn't know. In others she was with Dad. She'd aged by then; her hips were wider and her tummy stuck out. But her smile hadn't changed since the newspaper cuttings: a broad grin like in a toothpaste advert, but at the same time cold and forced. Dad had his arm around her and was smiling as well. I looked at his white, perfect teeth and realised I missed that smile.

In the last photos, the ones closest to the back, I began to appear. With my hair in bunches, or wearing my school smock, or dressed as a fairy. There were no pictures of me as a baby. Perhaps Julia had put them somewhere else, out of jealousy, but I doubt it. That made me sad, and I stroked my belly. I was going to take lots of photos of our baby, enough to fill a whole album. I put the photos of me and the photos of Dad on one side of the bed, then piled up the rest, the ones of Julia and of the two of them together, and put them in a bag. I returned the box to where I'd found it and replaced the hangers. Then I set about sticking the photos on the wardrobe. I covered the left-hand door with the ones of Dad and the right-hand door with the ones of me. I arranged them in date order, according to the numbers written on the back, and kept the middle door for when the baby was born.

Early the next morning, Dad was already dressed. He'd put on an old suit that was far too big for him, with the trouser legs rolled up so he didn't trip. The knot of the tie showed special dedication and he'd wet his hair and combed it back. It took my breath away to see him so handsome and full of life. He touched the lapel of his jacket with his right hand.

'How do I look?' he asked.

He licked two fingers and smoothed down his eyebrows. We laughed.

'Very dashing,' I said. 'Are you ready?'

'Yes.'

I'd left the fish tank outside and it was fun to keep him in suspense. I felt so happy! Inside me, the baby jiggled up and down.

'Okay. Since you said you wanted to see the water… Look what I got you!'

I went out and came back dragging the chair. The fish were still swimming around, oblivious, and the orange one was turning pirouettes. Dad didn't understand right away, and then, like a headless chicken, he carried on laughing for a bit even though his whole body had gone slack.

'Aren't they pretty?' I said. 'Look at the blue one, it's got a tail like a fan. We can buy some more as well.'

He was still standing in the same place, his eyes two tiny shrivelled nuts.

'Don't you have anything to say? Come closer, look at them.'

'You lied to me,' was what he said.

'What do you mean, Dad?'

'You're a liar.'

'Sit down. Please. Do you honestly think you could go walking along the seafront in the cold with wet hair? You can barely even stand.'

'Yes I can,' he said.

He took a few steps back, sat down on the bed and clasped his head, his elbows resting on his knees.

'No, I can't,' he said.

'See? Don't you realise it's for your own good?'

He didn't look at me; he shook his head to and fro in his hands, messing up the hair that a minute before had been silky and smooth as a slide.

'Who am I?' he whispered. 'Who am I?'

He was talking to himself.

I never knew exactly how many women lived in the flat next door. Their bedroom was adjacent to mine and at night you could hear voices mixed with music and obscene noises. They slept during the day and didn't start cooking until five p.m. When they talked in the bedroom I could hear most of their conversations, and sometimes I even stuffed my ears with cotton wool so I didn't have to listen to their filth.

It was late when the phone rang. On the other side of the wall, something crashed to the floor. Carmen lived directly beneath number 302 and was always calling me to complain about them stomping around, dancing and playing music.

'Those whorrres keep me up all night,' she said, her accent stronger than ever because she was angry and underslept. 'I'm going to rrreport them, the little bitches. They'll brring the rrroof down one day.'

When she hung up, she started banging back with her broom. Even I could hear her. She never called the police or the building manager, she just banged on the ceiling and telephoned me, whatever time it was, as if there were anything I could do. The women in 302 took no notice. The more Carmen protested, the louder they played their music. I never complained. I listened to them laughing hysterically and bumping into the walls like insects, and it didn't bother me.

The next morning, Carmen rang my doorbell. She had dark circles under her eyes and she was fuming, calling the women in 302 *disgrrraceful*. Again, she threatened to take them to court and got annoyed when I refused to act as witness.

'I don't like the police,' I told her. 'They get ideas and before you know it they're snooping around your house.'

Carmen thought I looked frail and asked if I was drinking the infusions. I lied. I couldn't tell her about Dad, about my worries over his mental state, and besides, I didn't trust her. She came inside, sat down on the sofa with her legs wide open and asked more questions about the baby: what I was eating, if I had the clothes and everything ready, if I was feeling tired.

'I'm not tired,' I said, and stood up to sweep under the sofa. I wanted her to leave, to leave us alone, and I almost swept her feet. She lifted them up and held them in the air.

'You don't look vell to me, dear. You're verry pale.'

Why did she always want to convince me something was wrong? Carmen was jealous because she'd never had any children, and now she was too old. One day she told me that the bomb which killed her father and brothers had left her with permanent injuries. In her uterus, she said, injuries that still hurt today. When she told me these things her eyes welled up.

'Is it that man?' she asked. 'Men aren't vorth our tears.'

'It's nothing. I'm just not sleeping very well.'

I opened the door and stood watching her. She got to her feet and laid a cold, rough hand on my cheek.

'It's not good to sufferrr over love,' she said.

At that moment, the door to 302 opened and the fattest of the women came out. Carmen looked her up and down with disdain. The woman barely acknowledged her as she strutted past, flaunting her broad, flabby hips. She was wearing a black miniskirt that revealed deep pits at the back of her thighs. Carmen pretended to be talking to me, but I was too on edge to play along.

'Looks like someone vas vorrking yesterrday,' she said, with a rasping, throaty laugh.

The fat woman paused halfway down the stairs, gave her the finger and then carried on.

'Dirrrty bitch!' Carmen shouted, leaning over the banister with her hair hanging down. 'Vait till I get my hands on you!'

She set off in pursuit, and when she passed the fat woman's door, she kicked the mat down the stairs.

I locked my door and put the chain on. My chest was tight with anxiety. It was twenty-four hours since I'd last seen Dad. I hadn't taken in his lunch or gone to check how he was. The fish tank was still in his bedroom, and I'd padlocked the window before I left. He must have been starving.

A bit later I went down to give Carmen my shopping list. She was still talking about the woman from 302 and her obscene gesture.

'How darrre she? You saw her, rrright? This time I'm going to rrreport her, I swearr. And good luck finding that doorrrmat, vherrever it ended up...'

Back at home I made spaghetti and boiled the vegetables. He'd been punished enough for one day.

The first thing I noticed was that Dad wasn't in bed. There was a horrible damp smell in the air, and I felt a strange sensation as I walked, as if the floor were cracking beneath me. I switched on the light and saw puddles everywhere. I thought Dad had forgotten to turn the bathroom tap off: he was in there with the door locked. It was a few seconds before I realised that the puddles on the floor contained pebbles and bits of glass. The fish tank was nowhere to be seen.

'Dad,' I said, banging on the door. 'What are you doing in there? Where are the fish?'

No answer.

I gave the bathroom door a kick and my leg cramped up all the way to my waist.

'The fish,' I yelled. 'What have you done with them?'

I looked in the puddles, which had spread under the bed, and among the broken glass. The fronds of seaweed were no longer rainbow bridges but rubbish bags left on the shore, and touching them made me feel queasy. I righted the fallen chair, where the fish tank used to be, and gathered up the biggest bits of glass. The canary was flapping non-stop in its cage. I'd never seen it so agitated, and it almost escaped when I opened the grille to remove the dead fish. The blue one was hard, its tail shrivelled and dry; the red one had been pecked all over and was covered in bird droppings.

There came the sound of breaking glass from the bathroom, and I think something inside me broke as well. In all that time, it had never occurred to me that Dad wanted to die, that he hated me enough to hurt himself. I threw down the fish and ran to the bathroom door.

'Dad, what are you doing?' I screamed.

I took a step back and then threw myself sideways into the door. I felt a stabbing pain in the right half of my belly and it hurt so much I fell to my knees. From the floor I went on banging with my hands and head. The door was shaking on its hinges.

'Dad, please, let me in.'

He must have been pressed up against the door, listening to me sobbing and resisting the urge to comfort me, because after a few seconds of silence, the door shuddered slightly and then opened with a click. I had to roll over to let him out. As soon as he saw me on the floor, he crouched down and helped me to my feet. I looked into the bathroom and saw a crack in the mirror and the sink full of shards of glass.

'I hit myself,' I said. 'I'm scared.'

We walked over to the bed, supporting one another. Dad didn't notice the fish on the floor and trod on one by mistake. His foot lifted automatically, but now the blue fish was mashed into the parquet, in a kind of transparent goo. We sat on the bed and I pulled up my top to have a look at my belly. A reddish bruise was appearing on the right, swelling into a tender mound. Dad ran his hand over the sore patch, barely brushing it, but his skin scratched me as if he had thistles for fingers.

'We need to call a doctor,' he said.

I shook my head and the walls started spinning. The bird lurched and crashed into one wall of the cage, then flapped its wings and regained its balance.

'Clara, you're bleeding.'

I touched my forehead and looked at my fingers.

'It's nothing,' I said.

Dad pulled at a corner of the sheet and pressed it to me like a cloth. We stayed there, not looking at each other, that cloth the only possible bridge between us. 'You hate me,' I thought about saying. 'You'd rather be dead.'

'Why don't you leave, Dad? The keys are in the locks. You could go if you wanted to. You could tell the rest of the world about all this.'

He didn't answer, just lifted the cloth slightly and looked to see if the cut was still bleeding.

'I mean it,' I said. 'The door's open.'

From that day on, he never mentioned the pier or asked to go out; he never said another word about it. It was as if he had suddenly understood something. Where could he go? His place was here.

The hob in the kitchen was on maximum. The flame grew taller and gave off an acrid smell when the first photo caught alight. I held it in the fire as it blackened and crisped. Then I put the remains in a bowl on the work surface and had to run my fingers under the tap because they almost got singed. For the other photos I used tongs, the same ones I used for serving spaghetti. I was nervous, in the way I always was when I did something related to Julia. The toothpaste-ad smile vanished, along with the Miss Springtime sash, the trophy, the silky dresses, the parties and champagne. All reduced to ashes.

Someone once told me that it's not good to burn photos of people, that it's witchcraft.

'You could kill the person in the photo,' a boy at school said.

I was killing the memory of Julia, erasing her forever from our past.

The smell of gas had filled the kitchen. The baby stirred, and I thought maybe it couldn't breathe. Wanting some air, I pushed open a window, and a sudden gust of wind got tangled in my hair. The flame flickered, blue, and I was scared it would go out, but when I shut the window it straightened up again. Once I'd finished the final photo, the bowl of ashes was full to the brim and for the first time I felt sure that Julia wasn't coming back. It was almost night by then and the sky was mottled like animal skin.

I went to bed early. My whole body ached and the bruise at my waist had swollen a lot. I was still thinking about the fish, and how pretty the blue one had been with its bridal train. Next door, a woman's hoarse voice was singing along to some music. I tried to make out the words, but it was impossible. I thought of the woman in the miniskirt and pictured her in her underwear with a microphone in one hand. Standing on the table, she wiggled her hips and gave off a horrible stench of alcohol.

After a while I realised the song was in another language and the voice was just a recording.

I wonder if wanting things intensely makes them happen exactly as we have in mind or just happen full stop. If it's the latter, I really might have killed Julia. I never wanted her to die smashed into a lamp post, or rather, I never thought about how I wanted her to die, I just imagined her dead: me coming home one day and finding her flat on her back, flies buzzing around her parted lips. I always had a sense that the flies would be the only outward sign she was dead. When she slept, she let her mouth hang open and drool would trickle from one corner. The whites of her eyes showed under her lowered lids and her breathing was so faint it was barely noticeable. Just as if she were dead; the flies were all that was missing.

But that wasn't what happened. Someone called me at work to tell me about the accident, and when I opened the door to the flat I found Dad collapsed in the dining room, along with two police officers and some other men in uniform. They were taking his blood pressure.

'He fainted,' said the man in white.

Now I'd never see the flies. Or the half-open mouth, or the trickle of drool, because her face had been destroyed by a lamp post. The car had flipped over twice before crashing into the post.

'Are you the daughter?' one police officer asked.

He was like an action doll, his muscles all puffed up under his blue shirt. He was trying his best to look sympathetic, and he spoke in hushed tones, as if his voice might make our pain worse. The doctor gave Dad a sedative and helped him into bed. They took me to identify the body.

Before Carmen told me what her father used to say about thoughts making things happen, it never occurred to me that I'd caused Julia's death. In the morgue I felt sure everyone was glaring at me, hating me, because I wasn't crying, but I didn't feel guilty.

'It's her,' I said.

I'd have known those purple varicose veins anywhere.

This image comes to mind: me on the rooftop. To my right is the end section of the church wall, where the bell tower begins. The bells aren't gold like in stories but grey or rusty brown, and coated with greenish pigeon droppings. They never ring, not even on Sundays. This makes me wonder if the church is cursed. No one ever chooses it for their wedding, which gives it a sad, useless air.

I want to reconstruct the view from the rooftop, to remember it so perfectly that I can't tell the memory from the real thing. The rooftop was my place; the only place where they couldn't get the better of me. To my left, the trees in the park resemble a green, even carpet. The buildings are low and look more like toys. To my right, behind the bell tower, more rooftops, clothes lines, TV aerials. Aerials like silver spiders. An invading army of spiders devouring the world. The streetlamps come on before the sun goes down; an orange thread suspended above the road. Behind the park and the buildings is the dome of another church, very different to the monster opposite. This one has a star on top, like a Christmas tree.

Wait. I think there was something else behind the dome with the star on top: a red and white metal tower. Or maybe I'm imagining it. Along with the church, the bells, the rooftop itself. Maybe I'm imagining it all. Dad and the bird are real, and Flor is too, and that's enough. I could say: one day Carmen flew in through the kitchen window; or say: her fingers had turned into great lengths of cartilage, there were feathers under her arms and she was foaming at the mouth. What's it to me? I've got nothing to prove. Only I know the things I know and nobody else cares.

I'm tired. I just thought about them in the other room and again I felt the weight of my solitude. How many million tons? The entire city collapsed to rubble on top of me. As a girl I used to like taking the labels off containers. I'd peel the stickers off shampoo bottles and then soak the gluey white residue, which collected under my fingernails. I'd rather think about anything else, just as long as I don't think about them. For example: shampoo that doesn't form a lather makes no sense. One day I put on conditioner instead and was rubbing for ages before I realised. If shampoo doesn't lather you feel cheated, as if you'd been sold a rotten piece of fruit. It's the same with life. Everything has its reason for existing and you just have to accept it.

Dad never understood that I loved him, and now he'll never find out. True, I never said so in as many words, but I always showed it. All I did for these past four years was take care of him, cook him vegetables the way he liked them, clean his room and bring medicine to him in bed. He cried a lot in the first few months, confusing me with Julia.

'Don't leave me,' he'd say, gripping my hand. He was nothing but skin and bone. Too weak even to make it to the bathroom.

I had to take everything to him in bed because he'd decided to stop getting up. One day he told me he couldn't sleep in the bed they used to share, that 'it swallowed him up as if the mattress were cursed', and asked me to put his stuff in the small room. For him I quit my job and moved into this dark, stuffy flat, and I even looked after the canary. There were times when we barely had enough to eat, but the canary never went without.

Dealing with the medicine man was another thing I did for him, to get hold of his sleeping pills, which you couldn't buy without a prescription. I knew the man from my office; he used to sell illegal diet pills to the women there and tablets 'for love' to the men. He always stopped by my desk and said he'd give me a discount, but I never bought anything. Which is why he was so surprised when I called.

The world is a bad place. The streets are dangerous and you can't trust the people. That's where Julia went wrong. And that's why I wanted to keep Dad safe, though he never understood. Until the day he died my father worshipped a world that robbed him of all he ever wanted.

.

Carmen stood over me clutching a kind of rudimentary scalpel, like a sharpened cane or a stake. Her white coat was more like something a butcher would wear than a doctor. The wide-open window seemed to be covered by an invisible cloth, because the air was stale and overheated. My lower abdomen was in agony: stabbing pains, cramps and a liquid running down my legs. I was about to faint. I held my breath, inhaled, exhaled, trying to remember Carmen's instructions. In the tangled web of pain, I heard a far-off voice shouting: 'Look at me, look at me.' The air squeaked drily into my lungs and I felt like I was breathing in the same gases I'd expelled a second before. Now and then, Carmen said things in her own language as she held my legs open with brute force.

'Keep looking at me,' she shouted.

I fixed my eyes on her sunken face, but I couldn't keep them still. They flickered from Carmen to the plastic palm tree and from there to the spotless white coat. The pain was so bad that I'd made a hole in the sheet with my nail-less fingers.

'I'm going to faint,' I managed to say.

Carmen's face grew deformed, her eyes spilling like eggs and her mouth a crooked line. That was the last thing I saw.

When I came to, it took me a few seconds to remember what I was doing in that strange room with a Mexican sombrero hanging on the wall. My vision was cloudy and the whole thing felt slightly absurd, like waking from an afternoon nap. The silence in the room was terrifying. I looked around and there was Carmen, sitting on a stool with her head in her hands, mumbling to herself. Then I felt a weight on my chest, looked down and saw a bundle wrapped in a bloodstained shawl. I couldn't bring myself to touch it. It looked like a snail and it wasn't moving. I could still feel a distant pain between my legs and had a vision of Carmen slicing me up with her implement. She noticed I was awake and looked at me, her face pale and bonier than usual.

'It's a girl,' she said, squeezing my arm.

'A girl?'

'The main thing is she's strrrong and healthy. And her lungs are definitely vorrking,' she chuckled. 'She's going to be an operra singerr.'

'I didn't hear anything,' I said. 'I fainted.'

Carmen got up and made for the door.

'I'll leave you two alone forr a vhile.'

The bundle whimpered and stuck one hand out of the shawl. It was a bendy, wrinkled hand, like the head of a tortoise emerging from its shell. I sat up with difficulty and put my finger in the curled-up hand; right away the tiny fingers closed around mine. I propped her up in bed and unwrapped the shawl, leaving her naked. There was mess on her legs and body, but her face was clean and pink. A girl. Now what was I going to tell Dad? I wiped her with the cloth, and her head fell backwards when I picked her up.

'Pretty thing,' I said, and she answered with the noise she used to make, back when she was still in my belly.

I nestled her against my breast, looking at her long, wrinkled baby fingers, and it didn't matter any more that she was a girl. When she started crying, I suckled her the way Carmen had explained. I don't think she drank much, she just tickled me with her bare gums. Carmen had told me it would be difficult at first, but it wasn't. She was always saying things like that to scare me.

We both began to doze off, although every now and then I jolted awake, afraid I was going to drop her. Suddenly I thought about Dad and felt worried; I hadn't left him any food or told him I was going out. Maybe I hadn't even opened the shutters.

I gathered up my belongings with one hand, and when I went into the dining room I found Carmen sitting in silence, her arms folded over her stomach. I thought she was asleep, but when my shadow cut into the lamplight she opened her eyes.

'Vait,' she said, getting up from the sofa. 'You need rrrest.'

She looked at the baby girl wrapped in the pillow case.

'Has she eaten?'

'Yes,' I said. 'I have to go home.'

Carmen took my elbow and tried to convince me to stay a little longer.

'You're veak,' she said.

'I can't. Dad's all alone.'

Carmen came the next day to see how I was doing. I felt empty, as if my insides had squashed up to make room for what had come and now they were stuck that way. My huge belly wasn't a pretty sight now the baby was out, so I bound it with strips torn off a sheet.

I asked Carmen to tell me everything from start to finish, because I had no memory of it at all. We sat in the dining room, the lamplight shining in her face and making her squint. Her elongated shadow took up the whole table: the head was right in the centre, over the vase, and it looked like a dark monster feeding on the flowers.

'She vas all pink and folded up,' she said. 'All crrinkly.'

'Like a flower?'

'Exactly.'

That day I named her Florencia. But we always called her Flor.

Dad didn't meet Flor until she was three months old. He must have heard her crying, but he pretended not to notice. I hadn't even managed to tell him she was a girl; he never let me talk about the baby, and if ever I began opening the door with her in my arms, he'd turn to face the wall and yell something at me.

'Don't you dare bring him in here! I don't want to see him!'

Flor had lost the hair she was born with and some funny dry patches had appeared on her head, like little grazes. Aside from that, she was plump and pretty. Pink, not white like those transparent babies that look like they're made of rice paper.

Were it not for his illness, Dad might never have met her. He'd aged a lot in recent months; he was thin, easily upset and his face turned purple at the slightest exertion. He was asking for more and more sleeping tablets. He also began to lose his hair. I collected it from the pillow and stuck it next to the photos on the right-hand wardrobe door. At first I thought he was pulling it out, but when he started to worry as well I knew he wasn't lying.

'I'm an old man,' he said. 'That's life.'

'You're just anxious, that's all.'

A few days later he woke up with a fever. His chest made a noise like a chainsaw and he frightened Flor with his coughing fits. I couldn't sleep. I ran from one room to the other, looking after them both: milk, nappies, aspirin. Soon the floor was littered with empty bowls, damp cloths and pots of vanilla yoghurt that Dad hadn't even touched. He couldn't swallow a thing. For two whole nights all I did was cover him up while he melted under the bedclothes. He pulled them off and threw them on the floor as best he could, but a few minutes later he'd be shivering with cold.

It was the beginning of February, and I moved about the flat as if swimming through the air or dragging thick chains on my feet. I don't know how many more nights went by. Sometimes I felt as if the ground had fallen away and I was sinking endlessly through space. One night I tripped over a rattle and spilt hot milk on my chest. Blisters formed like water droplets and burned when my nightdress brushed against them. Dad couldn't speak. His eyes were almost always closed, and when he opened them he looked at me like I was a trick of the light. I still don't know how I made it through that week. Sometimes, in my exhaustion, I forgot to breastfeed Flor. She cried and cried, but as I sank ever deeper into that abyss, her sobs would merge with a distant car horn and I wouldn't be able to hear her.

When I thought I couldn't take even one more night in that voiceless silence of tears and moans, Dad opened his eyes.

'Clara,' he murmured. I had to lean down to hear him, the sound was so faint. He took a breath and lifted his head very slightly from the pile of pillows. 'I'm dying.'

His voice didn't tremble, or his body or his eyes. He was firm and dignified. He spoke softly, his strength ebbing away, but the courage was still there, the same courage with which he had killed spiders and fixed exposed wiring as a young man. Nothing scared him, and Julia had never persuaded him to go with her to church. 'You mustn't be afraid of that stuff,' he used to tell me. That stuff being death and hell, Julia's great fears.

'No,' I said. 'Don't say that.'

'Yes, Clara.'

I sat down on the floor, next to his bed, and kept him company for a while. Dawn was approaching and the pale light had painted the church wall a speckled grey. He was still awake, but he didn't try to speak again. He sucked air into his lungs in loud, ragged bursts, and sometimes he seemed to hold it in and stop breathing completely. Then he'd close his eyes and release it slowly. He wasn't dying; he just didn't want to live. He'd decided to abandon us.

'You want to die,' I told him. 'I know you.'

He half-opened his eyes and looked at me through the slits, as if peering through the bars of a distant window.

'You want to leave me all alone.'

I rested my head on the edge of the bed, thinking I'd go to sleep, thinking I'd let him die once and for all, if he wanted to so much. The tiredness was overpowering and again I felt myself slipping closer to the edge of that bottomless abyss.

'Clara...' he said.

I shut my eyes, relinquished the last sliver of consciousness and let myself fall.

His fever gone, Dad went on coughing up thick reddish phlegm, but at no point did he ask me to call the doctor. He gave me the name of some medicine, which I bought at the pharmacy, and that same day, as I was supporting his head so he could swallow the liquid, he said he wanted to meet the baby.

'Let me see him,' he said.

'It's a girl. She's called Florencia.'

He seemed neither happy nor sad. He went on moving his lips, as if arranging the words inside his mouth, then said:

'That's a pretty name you've chosen.'

He received her sitting up in bed, without his beard. He'd actually asked me to shave him: he didn't want the baby girl to be frightened.

'She'll think I'm the Yeti,' he'd said.

Flor was wearing a white dress and pink tights. I handed her over, wrapped in a shawl, but didn't fully let go because he was still weak.

'How old is she?'

'Three months and two days. She was born on the 10th of November.'

I thought he'd be moved, but instead he burst out laughing. He laughed like he hadn't laughed in years. Flor squirmed, uncomfortable or overwhelmed, and dribbled a bit. Dad couldn't take his eyes off her, and I seized the chance to stroke his hand. He didn't pull away and I knew it was his way of telling me something.

'What's that on her head?' he asked.

'Some scabs, I don't know.'

'From dry skin?'

'Maybe.'

Flor started crying, and Dad got scared and shrank back like someone trying to shake off a spider.

'Take her away,' he said. 'I might infect her.'

He didn't see her again until July, and in the meantime he almost never asked about her. Sometimes I'd mention things, casually, because I knew he didn't like asking too many questions.

One day I told him Flor was trying to speak, but since she had no voice she just drooled.

'It's not that she doesn't have a voice,' he said. 'She's imitating the sounds you make.'

'She blows bubbles in her drool.'

'Good,' he said.

'What's good?'

'That she's drooling.'

'What do you mean?'

'I just mean it's good, because all babies drool. It's natural.'

'What about me? Did I drool?'

'Of course. You drooled like there was no tomorrow.'

We laughed.

'Do you think she'll start speaking soon?'

'You could speak before you turned two. You were a clever girl.'

I finished sweeping and collected the dirt in the dustpan.

'Stay a bit longer,' he said. 'Tell me more.'

I didn't have much else to say, but I told him a few stories, inventing details to make them more interesting.

'She likes biting a squidgy toy animal I got her, a frog. It makes a noise when she bites it and that makes her laugh.'

'How many teeth does she have?'

'Two. They're beautiful teeth, really white. Beautiful teeth like yours.'

'Is she eating?'

'Of course she's eating. She eats apple purée and other things I make. She likes eating. She eats everything I give her.'

'Don't feed her too much.'

'I don't feed her too much. She's really thin. She looks like a fishing rod.'

'And how many teeth did you say she has?'

'Two.'

'Two already…'

I laid my hand on his and rubbed it a little.

'You've got cold hands,' I said.

He seemed engrossed in the folds of the sheets that had slipped off his legs. Then suddenly he shot me a nervous glance and pulled his hand away.

'I'm tired,' he said. 'I'm going to try and sleep.'

That autumn I got into the habit of going up to the rooftop. I'd only left the building once since Flor was born, to buy camera film and a bag of birdseed. Carmen always did the shopping, but that day we'd had an argument and I didn't want to ask her. It was an argument about money, when she dropped off the bags from the supermarket and asked me to increase her commission.

'The bags veigh more every time, and I'm not getting any youngerr.'

'No raises and no advances,' I said. 'I'm not a bank, Carmen.'

She was furious.

'And vith all that cash hidden underr your mattress. You're so grrreedy!' Her tongue made a meal of the R as usual. 'You don't even have to vorrk...'

She set off down the stairs, still shouting, and I only realised when I opened the bags that she'd forgotten the film and the birdseed. Going out was becoming less and less appealing, especially now Flor had been born; it was even riskier out there with a baby. But I had no choice. Dad didn't want me to give anything but birdseed to that stupid canary.

I went over to the corner shop, carrying Flor. As we waited, the local old ladies surrounded me and thrust their heads between my arms. They groped at Flor as if inspecting a crate of vegetables, and although Flor didn't seem to mind, I felt a tightening in the pit of my stomach.

'That's eczema on her head,' one lady said. 'My husband has it too.'

'Poor darling,' said another.

51

'When her hair grows it'll cover it up, don't you worry.'

'If it does grow…'

'Now, now, don't be like that!'

They didn't shut up until the shopkeeper came back with my order. By the time I got home I was clammy with nerves. I waited for Flor to doze off and then started pacing around the flat. There was a horrible tingling in my legs, like electricity shooting up from my ankles. It was as if those old busybodies had got into the flat with their screechy voices and bad omens, and now I couldn't get rid of them.

I don't know where I got the idea of going up to the rooftop. I'd never been up there before, even though all my life I'd been seeing that metal door at the top of the little flight of steps. No one else in the building used it either, because you couldn't dry clothes up there or put out chairs or paddling pools. For safety reasons, said the sign stuck to the door. That first afternoon I went up without giving it much thought, never dreaming how important the roof would become. My space, my hiding place. From up there, everyone looked so small that they no longer posed a threat. Those old women from the grocery shop were nothing when seen from the roof, and the air was clean, free of the car fumes and bad smells from the street. The low wall around the sides had no guard-rail. I went almost to the edge, but kept my body further back than my head. I tried to guess how many feet I was from the pavement and had a sudden urge to jump. I imagined jumping and landing unscathed; imagined taking one huge leap that carried me all the way to the church roof. In the end I had to step back from the edge, not because I was dizzy, but because I was afraid of that ridiculous desire becoming too powerful to resist.

That afternoon, I wasn't on the roof more than ten or fifteen minutes. Later, as the days went by, I gradually persuaded myself it wasn't dangerous. I was wrong about that, but it would be a long time before I realised.

When I first took Flor up with me I made a barrier with my arms, in case she also felt the urge to jump. Sitting in my lap, she looked around wide-eyed. It wasn't the landscape she liked, so much as the brightly coloured laundry hanging on the roof next door. On windy days, the clothes thrashed at the air like whips; the trouser legs blew straight up in a V shape, then fell back down and got tangled in the line. The bedsheets danced like ghosts. Flor reached out her arms to them, transfixed. She laughed so hard that she choked, and I got the giggles as well.

But that was much later, once Flor had started walking. For the first few months, I went up alone. I was almost afraid of Dad finding out, as if going up to the rooftop were a kind of betrayal.

The first money-saving measure was disconnecting the phone. We didn't use it any more, and even if it rang I never picked up. I also worked out a way of cutting water costs right down; I only washed every three or four days and took Flor in the shower with me. But the worst was yet to come. Before long, showers, too, became a luxury and I started washing with a bucket and a soapy rag. By then I'd stopped buying disposable nappies and was even making clothes for Flor out of Julia's dresses.

Carmen once told me that during the war they'd been trapped, with no electricity or water, in the ruins of the city.

'A horrrible situation,' she said, her tongue vibrating against the back of her throat.

There were lots of them sharing a few jerrycans of drinking water, so they never washed and used cloth masks to keep out bad smells and disease. She was always telling me these things. Another time she said they wore their underwear the right way round for two days and then inside out for the next two. I remember because I found it revolting. I can just imagine them with handkerchiefs tied to their faces, their bodies stinking of filth and faecal matter like animals in a zoo. I was curious what animal Carmen would smell like. Skunks have a pungent odour, but you get used to it, and in the end it's not so bad. Not a seal, either, that would be too marine for her. Maybe she'd smell like Dad's bird. There was an undeniable similarity between the bird's feet and Carmen's stringy legs. Like the bird, Carmen balanced on two wrinkly sticks and then bulged at the waist, and her round eyes were so dark you could barely see the pupils.

Only now do I realise that none of it was chance. Carmen prepared her stories, and they all contained a message. It was the same with the building costs, which I'd stopped paying a long time ago, before Flor was even born. It didn't seem fair to have to pay that old bag who washed my front door with a dirty cloth and left everything dripping wet. Suddenly I'd hear what sounded like a dog sniffing at the door, open it and find the old woman plunging her cloth into a bucket of soapy water, the same dirty water she'd used to wash the staircase and all the other doors.

'I don't want my door washed! How many times do I have to tell you?'

But the old woman always came back. Maybe she was trying to hear something, to spy on us, though that didn't occur to me back then.

Carmen told me the building manager had spoken to her: the neighbours were complaining.

'I've asked him to give you a bit longerr, but vatch out vith that man, he's an animal.'

Money was becoming a worry and the only thing that helped was going up to the rooftop. But it wasn't the same going up with Flor, and by then I couldn't leave her alone. She was always touching things and could crawl at an astonishing speed. In no time at all she'd have her hand in a plug socket or be eating something disgusting from under the bed.

One day, Dad's door was left ajar and Flor crawled through it. I saw from the living room but didn't have time to stop her, so I ran in after her and picked her up. Dad was looking at her as if she were a stray kitten. I doubt he even recognised her: she'd grown a lot since the last time.

'Hello,' he said.

Flor was shy and hid her face in my neck.

'She's so big.'

'She's started crawling,' I said.

Flor peeped timidly through my hair.

'Go and see Dad,' I said.

I put her down and she stayed sitting on the floor.

'I'm in a hurry, I've got an errand to run.'

'You go, I'll keep an eye on her for you.'

'Are you sure?'

I locked the door and listened to Flor wailing for half an hour until I couldn't take it any more and went up to the rooftop. It was early July but sunny enough that I wasn't cold, especially if I stood against the wall, out of the wind. The flat surface of the roof was covered in metal sheeting and gleamed like an incandescent bed. The metal fittings, the door, the aerials, the water pipes, shot out strips of silver light that stung my eyes. I thought of Dad and Flor, together, and for the first time I felt as if we were a family. Things were changing. Before long we'd be like those families on TV, always happy. I pictured the three of us holding hands, walking and skipping along the edge of the roof, not afraid of falling or of wanting to jump. I pictured, in great detail, the drop on the other side. The people at the bottom looked like black dots and the cars like lines of matchboxes. I was scared, but my fear vanished when Dad took my hand. 'There's no way you could fall,' he'd tell me. 'Your mind's playing tricks on you.'

Back in the flat, I opened the bedroom door and found Flor sitting on Dad's bed. He didn't even say hello, just went on staring at the birdcage as if I didn't exist. The canary was asleep. That hideous creature slept more than any normal bird; it was nothing like a bird, in fact, the way it slept right through from evening until morning, unless the light was on. It made everything dirty and smelt weird and unnatural. The only birdlike things about it were the feathers and the pitiful little song it spouted every now and then. Once I stood for a while and watched it: it hopped from perch to perch, splashed in the water dish and cheeped away for the hour and a half it was in the light. As the sun moved, it huddled on the brightest side of the cage until it was pressed flat against the bars.

'Did she behave herself?' I asked.

I looked at Flor, who flashed me her usual drooly grin and reached out her arms to me. When I didn't move, she turned to look at Dad and made a gurgling noise. Her presence seemed more fragile than ever, a reflection that might disappear at any moment. I imagined her as a boat abandoned on the shore, with her body the anchor that held her in place. It was nice to know that she needed me so much, and a part of me wished she'd never learn to walk so I could carry her forever with her arms around my neck.

'What's wrong, Dad?'

He turned away from the cage, as if wrenching his eyes off it was painful, and looked at Flor instead. He lifted her up, his hands around her waist, and showed her to me. Her tiny legs paddled in mid-air, which made her laugh.

'This is what's wrong,' he said. 'God help us.'

Suddenly, the room expanded. I tried to lean against the wall but it wasn't there and I stumbled, my arm outstretched. The empty space bore down on me like an extractor fan, and it swallowed them as well. I saw them floating away, two grains of sand, just before I hit the floor.

Now and then I think I can hear noises on the stairs. Hard to be sure, because the silence is so total that it even has its own sounds. It's funny the way they managed to invade me in the end: from the inside out, planting the doubt like a weed. The reassuring part is that they won't be able to take any of what was mine. All they'll find is a wardrobe full of Julia's old rags, some worthless furniture and me, and I'm just like this flat: populated by dead things.

A door shuts on the floor below, or maybe it's out in the street, or next door, though it's a bit far away to be 302. A dull, abrupt thud. It makes me jump, but then I settle back down. False alarm. I wonder if this long, cruel wait is part of the plan, if this perfect silence broken by sudden noises is a form of torture, or if they're not yet sure what's happening in here. I'm cold, but I won't reach for a blanket. Flor and Dad must be cold as well, though by now they have no way of knowing.

I don't want to dwell on my defeat, but lying here it's impossible not to. I'm caught in my own trap: there's nothing left for me to do but wait, and I'm waiting. My thoughts turn to the police, and the day they first came to the flat. When was it? Before Flor turned one, before the horse. Yes, that's right, not long after I fainted in Dad's bedroom, because I still had the cut.

The policeman was short, with weathered skin like an old leather armchair. I would have known he was a policeman from a block away, even without the uniform. As far as I'm concerned, all the policemen in the world could be brothers; they move in straight lines and walk with a total lack of grace or flexibility, as if they were being controlled by wires from the sky. This one was so well-groomed that the entire hallway was left reeking of cologne. When I opened the door, he looked at me through the crack the chain allowed. The chain was exactly level with his eyes, so I could only see his mouth.

'Good morning,' he said.

His lips flapped like a dying butterfly.

'If you say so.'

The man stooped to look under the chain, and now the rest of his face was opposite mine. Weathered like a piece of leather, I thought. Young but wrinkled from so much sun.

'What happened to your face, ma'am?' he asked.

'What do you think happened? I fell.'

The cut was healing slowly because of the infection and had developed a horrible scab, a mixture of black blood and pus. In the mirror it looked like a cockroach had been squashed above my eyebrow, but it didn't really bother me. The policeman winced and touched his own eyebrow.

'It doesn't hurt,' I said.

'I'm sorry to disturb you, but I'm making some enquiries. The lady in 202, Carmen Diviak, said you'd be able to help.'

'I don't know anything,' I said.

'Have you noticed any aggressive or inappropriate behaviour from the residents of 302?'

'No, nothing.'

'Any obscene gestures?'

From the floor below came Carmen's howls:

'Just you vait, all of you! I hope you're all arrrested!'

'No idea.'

'Music late at night?'

'Nope.'

The fat woman in 302 opened the door and started screeching over the banister. Carmen strode up the stairs in a fury; the fat woman insulted her some more, calling her a witch. The policeman intervened and Carmen ended up behind him, trying to break free from the woman who was clutching her hair. He struggled to separate them, weary as an old horse, and threatened to arrest them both.

'And you'll go in the same cell,' he shouted. 'Understood?'

I could feel the policeman casting brief, brutal glances in my direction. His sharp eyes kept returning to my wounded eyebrow.

'So are you going to calm down?' he said. It was an order, not a question.

I closed the door and watched the rest of the scene through the peephole. They said something I couldn't make out and then the fat woman went into her flat and slammed the door. The policeman led Carmen down the stairs, resting a lifeless hand on her back.

From that day on I was afraid the policeman would return. Carmen might have told him about Dad or my problems with the building manager. I hadn't seen Carmen for ages; she only ever came to drop off the shopping and collect her payment. I wrote what I wanted on a piece of paper and didn't answer any kind of questions. This had turned her against me. I was brusque with her and made it clear that I didn't like people from outside my family. But the incident with the policeman had opened my eyes. The situation was more serious than I'd thought, and it was time to stop leaving the flat unless it was absolutely necessary.

I spent the rest of the day hearing knocks at the door and keeping watch through the peephole. In the evening I saw the policeman go into number 302. I'm sure it was him: the same smell of cologne and the same dark, fleshy lips. The fat woman opened the door and let him in. She was wearing a very tight dress that showed the fat around her waist. There wasn't much light in the hallway, but I saw his hostile glance at my door. They went inside. Amid the laughter and voices, I could hear him braying.

The next day, I decided to ask Carmen to leave the shopping outside the door from then on and knock three times to let me know. Her money would be in an envelope under the mat. She looked at me, stunned, as if I'd just said something terrible.

'Vhat did I do, dearr?'

'Nothing,' I said. Her eyes twitched. 'It's just easier for both of us this way.'

When I think about Carmen I picture her as a termite, a seemingly harmless creature that infiltrates houses, gradually chewing through the walls until only the foundations are left and the roof caves in on the poor people inside. Or at least, that's how I understand it. When she told me what happened with the termites in her house in Lithuania, or wherever it was, I couldn't stop imagining her as that monstrous insect. She said they had to burn all the furniture because the termites had got inside it and they were scared they might start eating the floor. I would have liked to burn her like that, like a termite.

The policeman went into the flat next door several nights in a row. I saw him once, but I always recognised the smell of cologne and his tired, wheezy voice. I thought I'd better mention it to Carmen, even though she was still offended. She didn't believe me. She said I must have imagined it.

'It was him, I swear.'

'Surrely not. Did he speak to you?'

'No. I saw him through the peephole.'

'You can't see a thing thrrough that tiny hole. It must have been someone else.'

'It was him, Carmen. And you can smell him the whole next day.'

It's amazing how things have to hit rock bottom before you realise what's going on. Only now do I see that they chose a slow death for us, a slow death like this one. Two years ago I was still naïve and didn't understand, and now it's far too late. There's no going back. The plan was too subtle for me to spot before it devoured us completely. The women in 302, the policeman and the other neighbours played a part, no question. As did the cleaning lady, the building manager and even the people at the court. Every single one, of course, answering to Carmen the termite.

On the 10th of November I sent Carmen to buy a birthday cake shaped like a daisy, a bottle of Coca-Cola, some sandwiches and a wooden rocking horse on metal runners. I had to pay her extra, plus the cost of the taxi, before she agreed to bring the horse.

'I'm not carrting that contrrraption arrround!' she said.

I spent a fortune on Flor's first birthday, but it was worth it. I even had one of those candles that light up by themselves, a magic candle. From the kitchen I saw Flor go tottering towards Dad's bedroom door and push it open. This made me nervous but I let her go. Not knowing how he'd react when he saw her, I waited a few minutes before slowly approaching the door. And there was Flor, sitting on Dad's lap. He was talking to her in a tone I'd never heard him use before. He sounded like a frail, quavering old man, and vaguely reminded me of the homeless guy in the Santa costume who begged outside the shop, but it was the sweetest voice in the world. They were looking at the canary and he was explaining something about how birds sleep standing up. She can't have understood much but she was listening carefully, not taking her eyes off the cage.

'Tweet tweet,' said Flor, pointing at the bird.

I sat in the armchair in the living room and waited a little. I was scared Dad would send me away or get grumpy, but when he saw me coming in with the cake on a tray he smiled:

'One already?' he said.

'Yep, today's the 10th of November.'

'How times flies.'

He looked at the daisy-shaped cake with its special pink candle and said:

'A flower for a Flor.'

That was probably our happiest day together. It's a shame I couldn't fully enjoy it, but I was nervous and spent the whole time glancing at the door. I kept hearing drips around the flat and had to go into the kitchen and bathroom to tighten the taps.

'What's that noise?' I asked Dad.

'What noise?'

We'd just sung happy birthday and Flor had blown out the magic candle again and again. In the end she almost burst into tears because it wouldn't stay out, and I had to help her.

'That noise, can you hear it?'

'There's no noise, Clara.'

Dad finished cutting the cake and Flor held out a plate to me.

'Not right now, thanks.'

She started eating and got covered in whipped cream. Dad wiped her face with a napkin and polished off the strawberries she left. Flor only wanted the cream and Dad was already starting to spoil her.

'She has to eat the fruit as well,' I said.

'Leave her be. It's her birthday, isn't it? Here, try some.'

One thing's for sure: her present was perfect. Flor was rocking away until midnight. I wanted to put her to bed but Dad asked if she could stay up a little longer. They were painting on a plate, their fingers dipped in dulce de leche. Meanwhile, I was going back and forth to the front door, checking through the peephole to make sure our voices hadn't alerted the whole building and no one was prowling around outside.

I almost had a heart attack when Dad picked Flor up and carried her to the window. She held onto the frame and stuck her head right out. I told him to put her down immediately. I said it under my breath, so no one would hear us, but with the sharpness of a shout. He took no notice and went on pointing into the darkness, telling a story about the birds in the trees. The little birdies that can go anywhere they choose because they have wings to fly with. I considered threatening to bring the padlock, but my threats had stopped working a long time ago. Now he didn't care what happened to him: he accepted it all with such resignation that I felt like a heartless but ineffectual prison warder.

'What's wrong, Clara?'

He put Flor down. He was tired and had started coughing.

'Someone might come,' I said.

He tugged at my sleeve and made me sit on the bed.

'No one's going to come,' he said. 'We're buried alive here.'

If I'd mentioned it, Dad would have said I wasn't thinking straight. He once told me the brain is like a pot of earth, and the earth dries out and ends up rotten and crawling with bugs. That's why I didn't even mention it. But who could say now that I wasn't right?

A month after Flor's birthday, in the lead-up to Christmas, I ran into Carmen while taking the rubbish out. It was a Sunday afternoon, when she'd usually be at the Tent with the rest of her sect. But no: as soon I opened the door I saw her on the landing below, grinning at me with her termite face and signalling for me to wait. She came up the stairs two at a time and looked into the flat.

'Aren't you going up to the rrroof today, dearr? The veather's glorrious.'

I tried to hide my amazement, and stood in the doorway so she didn't try to come in. Flor wandered over with a soft toy in her hand. Carmen squealed when she saw her.

'She's grrown so much! Vhat a lovely girrl.' She crouched down beside her and said: 'Hello, Florrencia, I'm Carrrmen. Don't you rrremember me?'

She picked her up and the soft toy fell to the floor. Immediately, Flor burst into tears. She must have thought Carmen had come for her: whenever I told her off, I said that if she didn't behave, Carmen would come and take her away and cook her in her stew, which is why she was bawling now and wriggling like a puppy.

'She doesn't rrrememberr me,' Carmen said, putting her back down.

Flor hid behind my legs.

'Go inside, Flor.'

I gave her a little shove and closed the door.

'Vhere vere you going?' Carmen asked.

'To take the rubbish out.'

I held up the bag to show her. Carmen went with me down the first flight of steps, and before disappearing into her flat she urged me again to go up to the rooftop.

'It's a glorrious day,' she said.

I couldn't pretend any longer. Carmen knew all my movements and kept me under constant surveillance like a prisoner. By now, not even the rooftop was safe for me.

There were two things Flor was scared of: Carmen and the back room. The times when I didn't threaten her with being cooked in Carmen's stew, I threatened to shut her in there.

The back room is full of wooden boards, tools and empty boxes. To reach it you have to go onto the balcony overlooking the inner courtyard, where the neighbours hang up their laundry and from where you can see in through the kitchen windows of all the other flats. From the balcony, it's easy to watch and be watched. When I was little, the old couple on the first floor used to spend the whole day out there, sitting on some miniature stools. That's how we learnt that the old man wet the bed and left half-sucked sweets all over the place, because his wife used to call him a 'dirty, disgusting old man'. If you went onto your balcony, it was almost guaranteed that the rest of the building would know all your private business. Dad and Julia used to sit out there to eat quince pastries and drink mate. The moment she saw them, Carmen would go out as well and lean on the railings to make shouted conversation. They talked about the weather and even exchanged recipes. Julia always smiled at her kindly, but as soon as they came inside, she and Dad would burst out laughing and call her a scarecrow. Dad once said he'd never seen such huge hands, not even on a man. Julia, still wiping away tears of laughter, told him not to say things like that 'in front of the girl'.

The back room was always filthy. However much Julia swept, the dirt, dead insects and rainwater blew in through the gap around the door, which had only a metal hook to hold it closed. Now the door might as well be boarded up; it hasn't been opened in years. When Julia died, I had the lock fixed and added a padlock. The door to the balcony is also kept shut and covered by a check blanket that serves as a heavy, permanent curtain. The balcony has always been out of bounds, and Flor would never have dreamt of going near it.

I expect there are some truly horrible things lurking in the back room to this day. Maybe that rustling I can hear right now is a rat burrowing under the floor. Someone once told me that animals change over time, mutating into malign species that humans can't control. I saw a film about it when I was at school, and afterwards I couldn't sleep for weeks. But what should I care about those monsters now, those deformed rats that have probably gone blind from living in the dark and developed thick tough fur like wire wool? In fact, it's fun to think what a fright Carmen will get when she opens the door and all those disgusting beasts hurl themselves at her, ripping out her eyes and ears with their long-famished jaws. It's a comforting thought: that there'll be some kind of reckoning and the creatures of the night, my creatures, will do away with Carmen and her sect.

I was just thinking about Flor's first birthday and how it was the happiest day of our lives. And it was, but it also marked the beginning of the end. In the months that followed, we had less and less money and felt ever more besieged. They cut off our water. I told Dad there was a burst pipe in the bathroom and I'd had to turn off the mains. He didn't ask any questions and switched to washing with the bucket of water I heated up for him in the kitchen. I didn't let myself wonder what would happen when Julia's money completely ran out. In fact, I never saw it as a real possibility, as something that could happen to us in the not-too-distant future. If I considered our situation at all I did so tangentially, skimming over the consequences, as if analysing an object that had nothing to do with me. And that's what this was, for more than a year: a possibility as alien and remote as everything else that happened on the other side of the window.

It sometimes seems absurd that time keeps on passing. Now, for example. It seems absurd that there doesn't come a point when time stops short. Like those people who thought the Earth was flat and there was a line where the ocean ended in a big waterfall. An eternal waterfall. Maybe the Earth is only round to stop people going to the edge and jumping into the void, to leave us with no way out. But time went on passing in spite of me, in spite of us, though it should have ended the day Flor turned one, with Dad's smile and the magic candle. That really would have been a happy ending. A perfect ending.

Gradually, I stopped going up to the rooftop. I went a few times in the summer and then less and less, until I finally accepted it was too dangerous. I hardly ever saw Carmen: the bags at the door, the money under the mat and that was it. Flor turned two; we celebrated with a dry sponge cake with chocolate icing and some coloured sweets stuck on top, and two ordinary candles. Then it was summer again, the final summer, although I didn't know that.

It was around that time that Dad asked me to move Flor's toys into his bedroom.

'She gets bored, being alone so much, and I get fed up, too.'

I took him all the toys: the horse, the teddy bears, the squidgy animals, the play kitchen, the Hawaiian Barbie. Dad said he'd never dreamt she had so many.

Flor was spending more and more time with him. Almost every day I made up some excuse to be alone – errands, paperwork, the problems with the pipes. I put out some food for them in the bedroom, changed the bird's water and left.

'I won't be long. Behave yourselves.'

Dad didn't look like he minded, but he didn't look happy, either. At first Flor tried to get out, she scrabbled at the door or called for me, sobbing, but I didn't open it. I kept quiet so she'd think I'd gone. In fact, I didn't go anywhere: I just sat in the living room, closed my eyes and thought about the rooftop, piecing the landscape together in my memory like someone fixing a broken vase.

At siesta time, Dad told Flor stories. Halfway through the story she'd fall asleep, and Dad would carry on a little, until he was sure she wouldn't wake up. Sometimes he dozed off as well, next to Flor, and I'd hear his loud, fitful breathing from the living room. It was always disappointing, because it meant I wouldn't hear the end of the story. Every afternoon I sat on the floor outside his bedroom door, waiting for him to pick up where he'd left off the previous day, but he never told the same story twice. Sometimes his voice grew so faint that I had to edge even closer to the door, taking care not to touch it, keeping so still that my muscles cramped up. Once I tried holding a glass against it. I don't know who told me about that technique, but it didn't work: all I could hear were distorted voices, like floating echoes in a cave. Those muggy afternoons, with Dad's voice swelling to fill the silent flat, and my own stiff, aching body, are the clearest memories I have of that final summer. Stray moments of calm that allowed me to forget, however fleetingly, the rooftop.

The heat clung to us like a damp cloth. The air grew humid inside the flat and there was no getting rid of the bird smell. People in the building left their doors open for ventilation, and the sounds of conversations and shouts, clattering dishes, radios, TVs and the ringing of the odd telephone all mingled together in the corridors, steeping in the putrid air that stank of greasy food.

Dad was having trouble breathing and his cough had got worse. Even the canary's wings had turned brown, withering like leaves.

'It's suffocating, the poor thing,' Dad said one day, looking anxiously at the cage.

Christmas wasn't far off and I thought I'd get us all a nice present, something to cheer us up. I wrote *Two cheap fans* on a piece of paper and slid it under the mat. I knew it was crazy. The termite made me pay for the taxi again, but I didn't care.

The fans brought us some relief. I spent almost all day in front of mine in the living room, and Dad sometimes aimed his at the bed and sometimes at the canary. They weren't very high-tech; they vibrated so much that by the end of each day they'd moved a few inches across the floor and they rattled like old fridges, but nonetheless,

Flor was transfixed. On the first day, she sat at my feet and put her face right up to the grille, so her voice shook.

'You're a robot,' I said.

This was a new word for her and she started repeating it non-stop.

'Robotrobotrobotrobotrobotrobot.'

I leant back in the chair with my eyes shut and tried to block out the sound. The days were getting longer and all I could think about was the rooftop, the low slender wall around the edge and me balancing on it like a tightrope walker, always about to slip. I saw the red sun hidden behind the bell tower and the roofs of the houses like a glittering staircase I could climb up into the sky. Flor's voice was stabbing at my eardrums, and I was trying hard not to lose my temper. Ever since I stopped going up to the rooftop, I'd been distracted and kept getting annoyed with Flor for trailing me around like a guard dog. She'd ask me questions and I wouldn't hear her, and then she'd repeat the same thing again and again until she shook me from my thoughts of the rooftop. It was always something unimportant: horsey, water, wee-wee.

'Robotrobotrobotrobotrobotrobot.'

I opened my eyes and sat up in the chair.

'Stop saying robot!'

Flor turned around and looked at me steadily. The rattle of the fan could be heard once more, a relief as slight as that fake breeze that barely reached our skin, then Flor's voice came buzzing back.

'Hellohellohellohellohellohello.'

Ever since I was a girl I've hated summer. The city empty and each night a gaping void. Outside the window, I'd hear the rustle of leaves and the whistling of the wind;

the balcony door would be open to let in some air, but that same air made the shutters creak, and I could never be sure there wasn't a rat in my room, or a bat, or one of those burglars who climb onto the roof and then slip in through the window.

'They stuff a rag in your mouth and then kill your whole family,' a boy at school had told me.

That was how I spent each December and January: waking up through the night and imagining where I could hide if someone came in through the window. Under the bed, inside the cupboard, behind the door. In February Julia would take time off, and we'd load up the car and go to the beach house. We rented it for the whole month, but almost always came back early because Julia was in a bad mood. She complained about the sand getting into the bed, the heat, the smell of the pillows, the mosquitoes.

A few houses away from our holiday home there lived some children who used to ride around on bicycles and attack me with water bombs or balls of wet sand.

'Why don't you go and play with them?' Julia would always ask.

One afternoon she made me wait in the garden while she and Dad had a siesta. The whole gang rode past at top speed and bombarded me: a ball of sand hit me in the back and I almost started crying. They pedalled away, hooting with laughter, and disappeared round the corner. Then a car drove by and sent up a cloud of dirt: it was a gravel road and the tyres made a horrible crunching noise, as if the earth were splitting open beneath them. Because of that, I didn't hear them approach. When the dust cleared, the gang came out of nowhere, shrieking like savages and pelting me with more balls of sand.

On their third trip around the block, one of the kids skidded on the gravel and fell off his bike. I watched him tumble into the verge and vanish in the brown dust kicked up by his wheels. None of his friends came back to help him; they were too embarrassed to stop right outside my house. I don't know what happened after that; all I could hear in the confusion were his howls. I thought he was dying, with thousands of those tiny stones under his skin. Dad came out to see what all the fuss was, and when I asked him what was going to happen to the boy, he said they were going to chop his leg off as a punishment for upsetting me. I thought that served him right, and felt sure my dad had had something to do with ensuring justice was done.

On the corner there was an abandoned house. I discovered it a few days after we'd arrived that first summer. The grass was tall and unkempt, and the blinds were pulled low; there were metal bars at the window and the wall beneath was stained with a crusty reddish trickle. I liked playing there. I pretended it was my secret world, a palace left standing after a war of which I was the only survivor.

The next year, when we went back to the seaside, the house was still uninhabited. Thick moss had made its way up the walls, and white mushrooms with enormous caps had sprouted at each corner. The gate had rusted; the black paint was all gone, leaving red dust that clung to my hands. The façade had begun peeling, too, and bits of plaster were falling off. I hit a bulge in the wall with a stick, pulled off some plaster and used it as chalk to draw a hopscotch grid. The anthills around the abandoned house were huge, too big to stamp on, so I set fire to them instead. Before setting them alight, I put stones in the holes so the ants couldn't flee to safety. Setting fire to an anthill isn't as easy as it looks; you have to stuff it with dry leaves and pine cones because the earth doesn't catch alight by itself, and even then the flames never last long.

Julia hated me playing at the abandoned house and sometimes she said as much to Dad.

'She spends all day in that dump when she has the whole beach to herself. Why do we even bring her to this paradise?'

Dad let her speak and didn't respond. Sometimes he chuckled, held the flat of his hand to his forehead and said: 'Yes, Sergeant', or 'Yes, General'. Then Julia would get annoyed and could go several days without eating or saying a word.

Gradually, as the summers went by, the house on the corner was transformed. They were small changes, and no one else would have seen it as anything other than a simple abandoned house, but for me it had become the only image of ageing I could understand. One day I'd turn up, I thought, and there'd be nothing there. Not because the house had been demolished, but because it had disintegrated by itself, leaving only a heap of white dust in the tangled undergrowth. When I asked Dad why nobody lived there, he said the house was so old it was beyond repair.

I often looked at Julia like that, as something old and beyond repair, and tried to spot some sign of her decay. But she was always the same, and her friends would even say to her: 'Julia, you never change a bit.' She had almost no wrinkles and her only insecurity was the varicose veins she'd inherited from her mother, fine as a fishing net behind her knees and thick as black ropes around her calves. A relief map of rivers and mountain ranges. That's the thing about decay: it can take a long time. Unfortunately for Julia, those varicose veins were all that survived the accident.

Someone once told me it would be impossible to relive everything that happened in one day, minute by minute, because the memory itself would take all day. I disagreed; I said you'd just experience two days in one. I'd like to put this theory to the test, but I think I have less life ahead of me than I do memories.

February, around midnight. I'd been keeping watch through the peephole since nine p.m. At a quarter to ten the policeman had arrived. This time there were two others with him. One young and thin, seemingly harmless but not to be trusted, and one fat, with a beard and moustache, and a feminine voice that seemed to come not from his body but from a transistor radio hidden in his clothes. The usual policeman rang the bell outside number 302 and the other looked at my door, sending secret signals with his eyes. They were each carrying a kind of canvas bag or rucksack. I shuddered to think what might be inside, maybe microphones or weapons. Frightened, I stepped away from the peephole, and soon after that I heard their voices on the other side of the wall. The music grew louder; they couldn't possibly hear us with the volume so high. There was laughter and a clatter of dishes. Then someone shouted over the music:

'The night's only just beginning!'

What began, however, was the banging of Carmen's broom, so hard it was making the floor shake. The women in 302 took no notice, and there would have been no point calling the police, so after a while Carmen gave up. By eleven there was no one left on the stairs. The man from 102 had gone off on his motorbike, as he did every Friday, and wouldn't be back before dawn. The other residents were all geriatrics at death's door who could barely get out of bed.

Everything was ready: the three plastic jerry cans and the wheelie shopping bag I used to transport them to the tap in the courtyard. As always when I went to steal water, my breathing had quickened and my hands were so sweaty they slipped on the handle. I picked the shopping cart up to carry it downstairs so as not to make any noise; I'd developed arm muscles from all that lugging it up and down. I looked around. No one. The tap in the courtyard made a screeching noise before the water came out. I waited for the slime from the pipes to clear and then filled the jerry cans. Every now and then I glanced over at the door and up at the windows of the inward-facing flats. The minutes seemed to go on forever and my heart felt tight in my chest.

When the last jerry can was finally full, I put them back in the shopping cart and got ready to go back upstairs. But on turning round I knocked the *Not for residents' use* sign off the tap, a metal sign that fell with a horrendous clatter, shaking the building to its foundations. I don't know why I didn't run. But I stood there like a statue, holding my breath, as if I could blend in with the plants in the courtyard. A few seconds passed, but no heads appeared in the windows. Not bothering to pick up the sign, I made for the hallway, pulling the shopping cart behind me and trying not to make a sound.

My sweat dried in the cool air. The shopping cart weighed a ton, but at that moment I could have lifted a sack of cement in one hand. I climbed up to the first landing with no trouble, but my problems weren't over yet. All of a sudden I looked up and found myself face-to-face with the old lady from number 101, who was wrapped in a white dressing gown and had curlers all over her head.

'What's all this?' she asked, clasping her hands in a prayer.

I hurried past without answering, without meeting her eye. She threatened to report me to the building manager, saying the maintenance costs were already too high for her to go subsidising everyone else. I thought she was going to chase me up the stairs, because she climbed a few steps, but then she stopped and shouted up the stairwell instead.

'How do you expect us old folks to get by on these miserable pensions, if you rob us at every chance you get? We never turned our noses up at honest work!'

Luckily for me, her chihuahua-like yapping didn't alert Carmen. Still, the termite would find out soon enough; just a few days ago she'd left a note with the shopping bags, telling me the building manager had filed the claim. It was only a matter of time.

Carmen had everything under control. I should have left the building then, when I still had the last of the savings and Dad wasn't too ill to get out of bed. That was the point of no return, and I don't know what held me back. The mere thought of leaving petrified me. I had no idea where to go and I couldn't imagine any other life than that one: the flat and my routine, taking care of Dad, cooking meals, cleaning the room, changing the canary's water, bathing Flor.

As soon as I shut the door, my body went limp. I felt twice as heavy as usual; each strand of hair, each fingernail, even the air that somehow made it in through my nose, all of it weighed me down. As I sat in the armchair in the living room, my arms still trembling from the exertion, my spine felt like an iron rod spearing me from end to end. I was only just realising how serious things were: I'd been found out. The building manager would cut off the water and within three days, if we were lucky, we'd have died of hunger and thirst.

That's what I was thinking when Flor emerged from
Dad's bedroom in her nightie.

'Flor, what are you doing awake?'

She half-closed the door and the light from the
bedroom shrank to a pale strip. The music in 302 hadn't
stopped and neither had the voices. Every moan was so
clearly audible that they could have been dancing right
there in the living room. Flor climbed into my lap and I
stroked her hair.

'What woke you up? Are you hungry?'

She shook her head.

'Wanna thee the birdieth,' she said.

'What?'

'Wanna go outthide. With the birdieth.'

'No, Flor. There's nothing outside.'

She started snivelling and rubbing her eyes.

'Birdieth…'

'That's enough.'

'Wanna thee the birdieth.'

I gripped her by the arms and shook her.

'What is it you want?' I shouted. 'Do you want to get
us killed?' She looked at me wide-eyed, on the verge of
tears. 'Do you want the ogre to eat you? To cook you in
her stew?'

She shook her head and began to weep inconsolably.
I had a terrible vision: Flor as a grown woman, knocking
my old, feeble body aside so she could open the door and
run into the street. I pressed her against me and felt her
damp face at my breast.

'Oh, poppet,' I said, hugging her tight. 'I'm sorry. You
don't understand, that's all…'

The sobbing didn't stop. I don't know if I was hurting
her, I just wanted to put her in my belly and never let her
out again, never ever.

I want to remember the last few months as one final stretch. No doubt there was a reason why the neighbour chose not to report me to the building manager or have the water supply cut off. I went on stealing water, more and more recklessly, because I assumed that everyone knew and I had tacit permission from the termite sect. Nothing happened just like that, and there was no point telling myself it had been a stroke of luck. Now that I'm a witness to our destruction and have nothing left to do but await the grand finale, Carmen's handiwork is clear to see. I understand, at last, that what they wanted all along was to throw me off the scent, to give me false hope so that sooner or later I'd let my guard down.

There came a point when all I could think about was the present. As soon as I woke up, the only thing on my mind would be how to get through the day. The war was being waged minute by minute; there was no space for making plans. We had to cling on through every moment until night fell. Then everything was different: Carmen's dominion faltered and we were able to regroup, ready to begin again the next morning.

Carmen and her sect had always had friends in high places. She often told me, proudly, that this country had been forged by immigrants. I could only assume she had secret government connections. One day, before Flor was born, I asked if she was interested in politics.

'That's men's business,' she hastily replied.

Then she turned away and started collecting the cups. The porcelain clinked in her hand and she didn't even complain that I hadn't finished my herbal tea.

So it was no surprise when our electricity was cut off. That was in March, but it was no less sweltering than January and the worst thing of all was not being able to use the fans. I asked Carmen for some packets of candles but made sure not to let on that anything had happened. In the evenings, although it was an unnecessary expense, I left a candle burning near the front door so that the glow was visible from outside.

The candlelight filled the flat with ghosts. The walls writhed as if they were being eaten by the flames, and objects cast long shadows that reached around the walls and ceiling. When the candles flickered, the flat was like an enchanted lighthouse, spinning out of control. At night I sat in the living room and watched the shadows until the candles burnt out and all that was left was a puddle of melted wax. When it got really hot I sat in the bath and stared at the shadow of the tap, with its long teeth like a helicopter propeller, but I never went to bed until all the candles had gone out.

Flor was scared of the candles. She didn't like being in the dark and her first reaction was to run away and hide under the table. She covered her eyes and waited, but when she peeked through her fingers the shadows were still there, snakelike and slithering all over the place. I crouched down and tried to coax her out.

'They're shadows, not ghosts.'

'Don't wanna.'

I had to get under the table with her.

'This is our little house,' I told her.

She laid her head in my lap and I stroked her hair until she fell asleep and I could carry her to bed.

In the nights that followed, her fear gradually gave way to fascination. She chased after the shadows and tried to catch them. She spun around, not knowing which to catch first, and sometimes she even got dizzy and sat down with a bump on the rug.

That was in March, or early April at the latest, because the court notice hadn't yet come. Someone slid it under the door, and I couldn't bring myself to read it until the evening. I left it on the table and eyed it from a distance, from where I could read the word SUMMONS in big letters. Once Dad and Flor were asleep, I opened it and checked the date when I had to attend, but that was it. I went to Julia's wardrobe, took out a pile of heavy blankets and draped them over the windows. I blocked the gap under the door with a bean bag shaped like a sausage dog. I stuffed toilet paper in the keyhole, and in the peephole as well. Only then did I feel safe.

On hot days I swapped the blankets for sheets, to let in a little more air. If it was windy, the sheets billowed out and Flor hid behind them and shrieked *Booooooo*. She could do that for hours. The flat, on those days, became possessed by the spirits of sheets. It was a beautiful sight, especially when the sheets inflated like lungs full of air.

One day we danced a waltz. It was only three months ago, but it seems like forever. Dad hummed the waltz and pretended to be playing the violin. I picked Flor up and we started to spin like the ballerinas on music boxes. Flor got dizzy and wanted to be put down, but I went on spinning and spinning because I never felt dizzy; I knew the trick of looking at my hand.

'Booooooooooooo! Boooooooooooo!' Flor had started playing ghosts again.

I told her to be quiet because I couldn't hear Dad's waltz.

'Let her have fun as well,' he said.

I let her, but we had to change games. Flor got bored of everything in no time; you had to keep changing or she'd burst into tears. The next game was Dad playing whichever instrument we told him to, and if he got it wrong there was a forfeit. So for example, if he was playing the violin and I shouted 'Piano', he had to switch to the piano. The idea was to be quick, so he'd get it wrong and it would be more fun.

'Trumpet!'

'Accordion!'

'Guitar!'

'Flute!'

We took it in turns to shout out an instrument, but I was better at it than Flor. She just repeated whatever I'd said. If I said 'Bagpipes!', she said 'Bagpipes' as well and then Dad didn't have to switch, so there was no point. I decided to whisper an instrument in her ear for her to shout, but it didn't work very well because my breath tickled her and gave her the giggles. One time I told her 'Horn' and she wouldn't stop saying 'Horn' for the rest of the game. I had to pull her hair because she was ruining everything.

'Horn's not allowed any more!'

But she carried on:

'Horn! Horn!'

The horn was a good idea. It was a difficult instrument to act out and Dad hesitated and played it like the flute. He argued that it was different because with the horn he didn't move his fingers and with the flute he did. We could never make him lose. Flor yelled 'Piano!' and he pretended to get it wrong. That made her laugh.

'Forfeit! Forfeit!' she cried.

'It doesn't count,' I said. 'He was cheating.'

If he'd lost for real, the forfeit would have been a week without the bird.

That was the last time I saw Dad with any energy. Like the abandoned house, Dad disintegrated slowly, piece by piece, but I didn't notice, or didn't want to. He grew too weak to eat or wash by himself, and the skin sagged hollowly at his cheeks as if he were sucking them in to pull a face. If I saw any of this, I didn't take it seriously; he was thin, that was all. I'd lost weight too and had even had to take in my trousers. But one day I went into his room and he didn't recognise me. It was just a few seconds; he looked straight through me as if I were made of glass, and then he was back to normal: 'Ah, Clara, you startled me.' That was when I felt, for the first time, that there would never be a future for us.

The night before going to the court, I dreamt that men in white coats were evicting us from the building. I went first and Dad followed, wrapped in a blanket and without any luggage. From the church roof, thousands of people were throwing stones at us and tipping buckets of sewage on our heads. I was running to and fro trying to dodge them, but when I looked up I saw a dark sloppy mass coming towards me. I jumped to the right but stones were falling there too, along with mountains of rubbish, and I had to jump again, forwards this time. Even though there was no way out, the slurry somehow always just missed me. I looked around for Dad and saw that the men in white were pulling on his arms and legs and he was coming apart without putting up a fight. Flor's voice woke me up. She said Dad didn't want to play. I went into the bedroom and felt his forehead; he had a fever.

'Leave him be. He's not feeling well,' I said. 'Come on, let's run an errand together.'

'Are we going to thee the birdieth?'

I said yes, and I also warned her not to mention Dad or else they'd put us in a pot and eat us like the giant in the story.

'Fee, fi, fo, fum, remember?'

'Yes.'

'Well, then. Behave yourself.'

Outside, the sun lashed at our eyes. The white stripes of the zebra crossing fired out shards of light like sparks, and Flor covered her face with her hands. I knelt beside the pram and pulled down the brim of her hat. There was a cool, mid-May breeze, but the sun was making me sweat in my woollen coat. I looked at the blue, even sky: not a single cloud to temper the onslaught of light. Pushing the pram, I made for the court. Flor gazed around as if she wanted to eat the whole world with her eyes, not realising it was the world that was going to eat her.

The court was in a big old building with a marble staircase. As soon as they saw me go inside, two men came down the steps and reached for the pram.

'I can do it myself,' I said.

I made it up a little way, but then it was too steep.

'Allow me,' said the older man.

'I'll help,' said the other.

At first I refused to let go, but eventually they took hold of the pram in front and behind and carried Flor up the steps. I followed them closely, ready to spring into action if they tried to run away with her.

In the waiting room, a man offered me his seat. To my right sat a young woman, as beautiful as the women on TV. To my left was an old lady with a walking stick. The young woman shifted in her seat, edging slightly away from us. Her eyes lingered on me and Flor in silent judgement. Nothing about our surroundings filled me with confidence, and those figures may as well have been Martians. I got to my feet, my mind made up, and pushed the pram towards the exit, but before I was down the first step the men were hurrying over with their solicitous, extraplanetary smiles, ready to stop me. They were ruthless gatekeepers: I realised I had no choice but to stay in the court and wait, without attempting any movements.

The judge turned out to be a woman. She made me sit down and spent a few minutes talking to Flor. She asked her what her name was and how old she was.

'Two and a half,' I said.

'Would you like a lolly, Florencia?'

Flor nodded; she'd stuffed four fingers into her mouth.

'Lemon or strawberry?'

'Thtawbee,' she said, dribbling down her hand.

The judge's eyes were like silent trees, filled with all the evil of forests. They settled on me with false benevolence and assessed my hair, my clothes, my bitten nails. The level of planning made my blood run cold. Every detail had been thought about in advance: the lolly, the chair and the guards on the steps, who thought they'd invented good manners.

Julia's money had run out. There was almost nothing left of the savings hidden under the mattress; enough for two or three months at the most. The judge talked a lot that afternoon. She never raised her voice; her monotonous drone clogged up my ears and only managed to confuse me. All I understood was that I had to pay the overdue building costs.

'You're almost three years late,' she said, leafing through a white notebook tied up with string. 'Plus interest...'

She read out a list of dates and numbers which I barely heard, and which meant nothing to me in any case. Whether it was three million pesos or thirty, there was no way out for us.

'Do you work?'

'No.'

'And the girl's father?'

An avalanche of accusations, as if she had the right to stick her nose into our business. I knew it: one day they're asking questions and the next they're inside your house, taking your stuff, making decisions, and they don't have a clue what they're doing. I was powerless to resist. My face was burning and I was struggling not to cry. And most humiliatingly, most unforgivably of all, I had to mention the medicine man in front of Flor.

'So in other words, the flat would need to be sold to pay the debts. Do you understand?'

I said yes and looked at Flor. She didn't understand. Silently, without moving from her pram, she turned the lolly over inside her mouth.

'We'll call you in again,' said the judge. 'Please be sure to attend.'

We were in there hardly any time at all, but it had a devastating effect on our lives. I got home drenched in sweat and my teeth hurt because I'd been clenching them so hard. I sat Flor between my legs in the big bed and we ate meringues, showering the bedspread with crumbs. She just sucked them and melted them with her tongue. I gulped them down almost without chewing, as if that might shake loose whatever I had lodged inside me. Flor left the last meringue half-finished and fell asleep. I ate the remains, and then, in a sudden frenzy, I kissed her sticky, sugary hands. I licked her sweet little fingers, rubbing them clean against the roof of my mouth, and then I kissed her head and I kissed every single scab that poked out through her hair. Flor didn't even wake up.

I want to believe this is a calm, cloudless night. One of those nights when the moon is so big and bright it's as if you could touch it, and you worry it might fall out of the sky.

It's odd that the sect chose July as the month to deliver their final blow. Only Carmen, who knows us well, could have come up with such a sick joke. Julia's accident also happened in July, and I admit that at the time I found it funny. Julia, July. Never mind; I doubt we'd have survived the rest of the winter with no electricity or hot water, or money for basic necessities. Food no longer warmed us up, because the cold had become a presence in its own right. The rooms had turned into wastelands, and even with furniture they seemed barren. We breathed clouds of steam from our mouths and noses like human locomotives. Flor laughed every time a white cloud plumed from my mouth, especially if it happened when I was telling her off. I felt more lethargic than ever and tried to speak as little as possible.

Along with the cold, the silence in the flat was seeping into my bones. The memory of the rooftop would come crashing down on me like an avalanche; it hit with the same cataclysmic power and froze me from head to toe. Sometimes I even had dreams about the rooftop, almost always nightmares: stepping onto the roof and it crumbling beneath my feet, collapsing on Dad and Flor. Or stepping onto the roof and finding it covered in dead fish, with a giant bird, half-canary, half-vulture, pecking out their eyes.

After the court hearing came some blustery weeks. They say people go mad in windy places, and now I understand why. It plants something nasty in your soul, a kind of malignant disquiet. Sleep became impossible; all night long I heard drips and footsteps, tossing and turning in bed. The wind made me into a nervous wreck, and when it went it took what little sun was left and sent back the bitterest winter. It happened just like that, from one day to the next, or that's how it felt to us because we had no way of getting warm.

Not long ago, on a freezing night like this, I woke up with my heart racing. I'd fallen asleep in the armchair, my head tilted back, and I'd had another nightmare. The candles were still alight; they didn't melt as quickly as in the summer months. It was two in the morning and the building felt dead. On such cold nights the policemen didn't visit the den of iniquity at number 302, and no one ventured into the corridors. Not so much as a sigh could be heard through the wall; the women in 302 must have been huddled under the covers, feet slotted together for warmth.

I'd had another dream about the rooftop: pushing open the door and finding a pile of naked corpses, women, old people and children with no teeth or fingernails, all skin and bone like in those photos of wars. Dad was among them and I had to find him, gingerly extracting the malnourished bodies as if it were a game of pick-up sticks.

I got up from the armchair and walked around the flat, not sure what I was looking for or why. I felt only very slightly, very hazily awake. Flor was asleep in my bed, as usual, and Dad's door was closed. I opened it a little way and looked through the crack; the candle had gone out and the only sound was the hoarse, fitful rattle of his breath. I carried on towards the bathroom and looked at my candlelit reflection in the mirror. I'd let my hair grow. My body hair, too: it was months since I'd shaved and my legs and armpits were covered in long, soft strands that curled at the tips. Even my eyebrows now met above the bridge of my nose, bristly and irregular. All this together gave me a primitive look that protected and separated me from other people. Which was fine, but nonetheless, I hardly recognised myself. A pale, ageing face that seemed covered in mildew. An invalid's sunken eyes.

I hurried back to the bedroom and put on the woollen cardigan I'd been using as a blanket. It was orange and floor-length, and had been Julia's favourite. She paraded around in it, showing off, making it twirl like a gown. I'd only ever used it as a blanket, and when I put it on it felt heavy and artificial, almost like fancy dress. I didn't think about what I was doing, not even when I opened the front door and climbed the metal steps to the rooftop.

The cold was the dry kind that cracks your skin, and the doorhandle was frozen. I pushed at the door with both hands; the creak echoed through the corridor and then faded. Right away, the cold forced me back. I stood flat against the door and looked at the black strip of sky. In the distance you could make out the glow of tall buildings; a fantasy world, because in this neighbourhood there was only one streetlamp on the main avenue and another on my block, and that one didn't even work. Now and then the light reached me from passing cars. When they were gone, the roof under my feet merged with the night air and the low wall melted away. Where did the roof end and the void begin? I'd have liked to see the moon as I imagine it now, round and immaculate, lighting the whole flat, but that night the moon was hidden behind some clouds scarcely brighter than the rest of the sky. The night turned the roof into a sinister place, and standing there, in my domain, with my creatures, was a victory and an act of defiance.

At first, I didn't have the courage to move. Then my eyes began to adjust and I was able to distinguish a few shapes: the great stain of the church wall, that dark fleshy shoulder that turned the rest of the shadows black; the clothes on the washing lines; the TV aerials; my own moon-silhouette. I took a deep breath. The cold scorched my skin like dry ice, but that frozen, lacerating fire seemed to have travelled thousands of years just to reach me, just to cleanse me of all that was evil and vile, and make me into somebody new.

Julia's cardigan blew out to one side, snapping in the wind like a flag. I put my hands in my pyjama bottoms to protect them from the cold. I wasn't wearing any underwear and I could feel the warmth of my pubis. I stroked the soft fur that had spread to my inner thighs and up to the beginning of my stomach. The streets were empty. I didn't think I'd ever seen them so silent and deserted, and I felt like the only person in the city. While everyone slept, defenceless in their cosy beds, I reigned supreme, the queen of the night in my red cape. I straightened my shoulders and pushed my hands deeper between my legs. Carefully my fingers unstuck the lips and found a damp, sticky heat. Rising higher and higher, above them all, above the trees, the streets, the cars, I suddenly understood the meaning of things, the secret power they contained. Unhurried, unafraid, I closed my eyes to feel the night air on my face. I knew something that other people didn't, and at that perfect moment, when all the pieces of the night seemed to slide into place, I opened my eyes and saw the vast moon emerging from the smudged grey clouds. It was an old man, the round face of an old man in the middle of the sky.

When I returned to the flat it was almost four and I went straight to bed. That was my last visit to the rooftop.

I want to know how I ended up here; what initial image or thought it was that made everything come back. When did all that happen on the rooftop? A week ago? Two? I don't know, and I don't know if it matters. What are weeks, anyway? Just a number. Another meaningless number. How many weeks make four years? How many days? Three hundred and sixty-five times four. I can't do the maths. I'm cold and I think it's nearly dawn. Before getting into bed, I took down the blankets from the windows and left them folded in a pile on the chair. Julia's cardigan is covering me to my waist, but it's not enough and my feet are freezing. I could get up, take a blanket from the pile, but I'm not going to attempt to move. I wouldn't like to find that my body's gone dead and my hands won't do what I tell them.

I couldn't sleep last night. Maybe I sensed something. In the early hours I went into Dad's room, though I have no idea why. I'd woken up from a nightmare with a pounding headache. Someone told me a while ago that when nightmares are too awful they're impossible to remember. If we could remember them, I think we'd die. When someone dreams about dying they never wake up, they die in real life. Because no one dreams about dying; they might dream that they're about to die or that they're in danger, but those dreams never get to the end. I often dreamt that Carmen and other faceless figures were chasing me and wanted to kill me, but I always made it out alive. In one dream I hid under a rock, and when I woke up I couldn't stop laughing. Another time I dreamt about cutting Carmen's face up with a saw. I cut it lengthways, like slicing a lemon.

Sometimes dreams are premonitions. It occurred to me last night that perhaps the reason I couldn't remember the dream was that it contained a hidden message. I drove myself mad trying to remember it. But of course, trying never works. Whenever Dad forgot something important, Julia would say:

'Don't think about it. It'll come to you.'

What was worrying me last night was Dad's temperature. He'd been feverish every day lately, and not even a damp cloth could cool him down. But I gritted my teeth and stayed in bed a little longer. Julia always used to tease me if I got up in the night and went to sleep in their room. Came, I should say, not went, because they used to sleep in this room, in this bed, and I slept where Dad is now.

'There's something in my room,' I'd say to her.

Julia would pretend to be asleep and I'd stand by the bed, my legs squeezed together. Eventually she'd open her eyes, as if she hadn't heard me come in, and then, grumbling, she'd get up, take my hand and lead me back to my room. She'd turn on the light and we'd look around.

'See anything strange?' she'd ask.

'No. It's gone now.'

But then she made me check under the bed. I hated looking down there because it was full of fluff and forgotten objects that looked like dead insects.

One day she got impatient and made me run my hand under the bed to prove there was nothing there. It was disgusting; my hand came out black, with a clump of hair snarled around my fingers. I had to go and wash in the middle of the night, in the icy water that took hours to warm up. And so most nights I tried not to get out of bed, putting up with the fear as best I could.

Back then there used to be trees on the pavement. They were covered in leaves throughout the summer, so you couldn't see the church wall. In the daytime I was glad: I hated that wall. But at night the leaves shook and sounded like rattlesnakes. I'd wake up in the early hours and watch the shadows on the wall; they never stayed still, and sometimes I wondered if they were spiders, or burglars slinking through the dark. If they were burglars, the best thing would be to pretend to be asleep, so they'd take the stuff quickly and leave. But if they were spiders that might be dangerous. A tarantula bite could kill you before you made it to hospital. At school I'd learnt that the poison paralyses your lungs: you go purple, your throat swells up and the air stops getting through. In class we played at seeing who could hold their breath the longest. The record was one minute ten seconds. Not even two minutes or three would be enough time to get to hospital.

'What if you went in a helicopter?'

'You can't go to hospital in a helicopter,' one boy replied.

'Why not?'

'I don't know. You just can't.'

I was sure I was going to get bitten by a tarantula. Every so often I'd feel something crawling over my arms and legs, or inching up my nose. Sometimes it was a hair or a strand of wool from the bedspread, and other times it was nothing at all.

One day some uniformed men came in a truck and pulled the trees up by the roots. The trees used to produce these furry yellow fruits, which fell to the ground in spring and messed up the pavement. I thought that might have been why they were removed, but no. I later found out the authorities were worried about snipers.

'I don't know why they bother getting rid of the

trees, when they're the real murderers,' Dad said at the time, but I never understood who the guys in the truck had killed.

So last night, too, I held out as long as I could before getting up, simply out of habit. I waited until I saw the first glint of dawn, a glint only I could see because I'd become a connoisseur of the shifting light, then I went into Dad's room. The inhuman silence of a catacomb hung in the air. Not wanting to light the candle, I felt my way through the gloom until my hand reached the back of the chair. The bed was a few steps from where I was, and I could just make out Dad's shape under the blankets. I went to the cage and gave it a push to wake the canary. Whenever I shook the cage, the bird would untuck its head from its chest and flap its wings in alarm. Dad didn't like me doing it, and even if he was asleep he'd normally wake up and say something. But this time he didn't wake up, and neither did the bird. The cage swayed to and fro, making no more noise than the swings in the park. I peered through the darkness; the animal wasn't on the perch as usual but lying flat on its back, legs stiff and half-extended. Dead. A taxidermy bird.

Dad and the bird led synchronised lives. I thought I'd be able to avoid the topic of the bird and the synchronisation, but I was wrong. I can't lie to myself any more. At first I could practically hear myself saying, 'Please don't remember,' but at the same time, inevitably, I was bringing the memory back. Ever since midnight, when I lay down and covered my legs with Julia's cardigan, I've known I was approaching this dreaded moment. I suppose I was hoping they'd get here first. That they'd take me away and do as they willed, but quickly, before my mind could add the final full stop. Because after that, what's left? Am I really going to begin again? Am I going to remember in an endless loop, like on a round Earth there's no escape from?

I don't know how many hours have passed. It could be six o'clock by now, or seven. The church wall makes it difficult to tell, especially in winter, because it looks different depending on whether it's cloudy, rainy or sunny. There's a very soft glow on the bedroom wall, under the window. Seven-thirty, no later. The building's too quiet for this time in the morning, but today is a special day.

When I can't sleep, I think about the colour blue. I close my eyes and focus on painting everything dark blue. It soothes me, submerging me in the abyss of my mind until I lose all sense of my body. My hands feel hundreds of yards away; my legs tingle and I can't distinguish that state from genuine sleep. I don't know how many years I've been doing this, or if I've always done it and one night I suddenly realised. And I don't know why I chose the colour blue. When I've tried it with other colours in the past, it's never worked. On the nights when I thought about white, I could never get to sleep. One idea led to another, and I associated the white with the wall and the wall with the canary and the canary with Dad, or the white reminded me of Flor's socks, and then I remembered I had to buy her a new pair and that, of course, reminded me of Carmen, and then there was no chance of getting to sleep. If I concentrated on red or black, I had nightmares: wars, blood, toppling buildings. Only by painting everything blue can I sleep in peace. The next day I'm refreshed, as if I'd slept for ten hours, even if I had to get up five times to rock Flor back to sleep or check that I'd locked the front door.

I'm surprised, in a way, that it's not working tonight. I feel betrayed by my own brain; the idiot thing can't stop clutching at memories instead of listening to me, its owner. I don't think a single part of my body is still listening to me, in fact. And the worst thing is how much it hurts, even the happiest memories. Dad's smile hurts. Playing with Flor hurts. The stories, the caresses, the hands under the sheet, they all hurt. If I could get up, I'd gladly bang my head against the wall to stop myself from thinking. But I can't. It's all my fault that we ended up here; I should never have begun.

At around midday I went back into Dad's room. Flor ran to the bed, clambered up and straddled his legs. The room smelt foul. Not only from the dead bird, but from the dirt and stale air. After the court hearing I'd given up on housework, and sometimes went for days on end without changing Dad's sheets or emptying his bedpan. I didn't have any cleaning products, either, or enough water to flush every time we used the toilet. Rubbish bags were piling up in the kitchen, and only when they started blocking my way did I find the strength to take them out. I pulled back the blanket that covered the window and opened the shutters. A blast of icy wind freshened the air. The cage began to swing, with a creaking noise I found sinister. It was a sunny day.

Flor bounced up and down on Dad's motionless legs until he blinked open his eyes. His lashes tracing a slow, arduous semicircle, he looked around and finally his gaze landed on me. I'd spent all morning thinking about the canary, about its desiccated body on the newspaper and how I was going to tell Dad. My nervousness must have given me away, because I glanced at the cage despite myself. It was just a flicker of the eyes, but so despairing, so desperate for a miracle, that it was the only explanation Dad needed.

'Clara,' he murmured, which, thinking about it, was the last word he ever said.

I'd have given anything for that repulsive bird to get to its feet and start cheeping, anything at all.

'It's a beautiful day,' I said.

Flor had been crawling up Dad's legs to his waist,

and now she pressed her face to the folds of his neck. She blew harder and harder until she sounded like a broken trumpet. 'The cow sneezed,' she told him. Every morning Flor woke Dad up by snorting like that, and he'd withstand her tickling and pretend to be asleep, until her grunts became so frantic and her laughter so loud that he'd open his eyes and feign a horrible shock, as if he'd just discovered a cow was attacking him. Then he'd clap a hand to his chest, in a show of terror, and let his head slump to one side. Flor would shake him to make sure and then say:

'It's me, silly! I'm not the cow!'

He wouldn't react, playing dead a bit longer while she shook him and pinched his nose until he finally came back to life.

But this time Flor's sneezes met with no response. It was quite simple: the canary's absence had upset the routine. It's comical and dreadful to live in thrall to a canary. But it can be very real, more real than anything else. And then one day the bird dies and the circle of life in the flat breaks down.

Flor went on blowing raspberries into Dad's neck.

'Come on, you have to die now... I'm the cow!'

She put her lips to his ear and whispered:

'Dad? I'm the cow.'

With considerable effort, he lifted one arm and draped it over Flor's back. She waited a few seconds, but when she saw he wasn't playing she wriggled free of the embrace and climbed off the bed. I stayed sitting on the edge, and thought I'd better not mention the canary. I reached out and laid my hand on Dad's. His skin felt soft and feverish.

Flor was barefoot and skating around on a pair of old socks. She crouched next to the bucket of water, filled one of the plastic pots we used as water dishes for the canary and handed it to me. I got up and went over to the cage, as if nothing had happened. I opened the metal door and put the water dish inside. The bird's round, lashless eyes blankly returned my gaze. I sat down and rested my hand on Dad's again. Suddenly I felt lost, as if I were wandering in circles in an unfamiliar place, searching for landmarks I'd never find because I'd never been there before, but still trying, still believing. I wanted him to say something; after all, he was my dad. He may have been dying, but he was still my father and I expected something from him: some reassuring words, a promise that everything would be alright.

Flor came skating towards us.

'Put your socks on,' I said.

She squatted at my feet and threaded her arms into the socks, which came up to her elbows like princess gloves. She climbed into my lap and stroked Dad's face with her new gloves. They were dirty, the soles black with fluff, but I didn't say anything. She'd started talking in her doll language, a mumble that had no meaning but brought us some relief. Flor filled the silence that separated me and Dad, a silence that had begun four years ago. Just then, he squeezed my hand. Hard, with the last of his strength. I squeezed back but couldn't bring myself to look at him. Dad had always been a mystery to me, and now he was squeezing my hand and I didn't know what it meant, what any of our time together had meant to him.

We stayed in his room for the rest of the afternoon. We didn't talk about the canary or what was happening because there was no need. The corridor outside was buzzing with activity; their preparations were underway.

I heard them scurrying up and down the stairs, singing under their breath and laughing in the shadows. Maybe they thought I didn't know. I enjoyed every minute of my lack of anxiety. I imagined Carmen clapping her hands like saucepan lids and shouting orders left, right and centre. The policemen were there too, probably lined up on each side of the staircase. They'd want an important role in the procession, the crowning event of their lives.

The three of us − me, Flor, Dad, in that order − formed a chain of hairdressers. Flor stood in front of me and I gave her two plaits; she messed up Dad's hair and tried out various styles. It was easy because his hair was so dirty that it held whatever shape you gave it. We worked in silence, not out of fear of being heard but because the task required great concentration. Dad's head was like a nest: the hair around his ears stuck out in all directions and it was tuftier than usual at the front.

'Your head's like a nest,' I told him, and then asked Flor: 'What's Dad's head like?'

'A netht!'

We laughed. Dad's breath was so faint that sometimes he didn't seem to be breathing at all. But yes, there was life in him, I knew without needing to lean over and take his pulse, without needing to fetch the little mirror. A living person isn't the same as a dead one, I've learnt. What leaves is too big to pass unnoticed.

Bees live in hives, those brown nests that hang down from trees like stalactites. When there's no queen bee, the swarm disperses and abandons the hive. I don't know what bees do when the queen dies, but I've heard they scatter and start flying in all directions. Perhaps many of them die or get lost. Why am I thinking about bees right now? Right from the start, I thought I was the axis at the centre of this household. It's not that I considered myself more important, but without me they wouldn't have lasted a week. Carmen would have gobbled them up in the blink of an eye. I knew my mission and I fulfilled it to the last. Maybe it's pointless to be proud of that now, but it's helping me face up to Carmen and her court, whatever the sentence might be.

I've learnt that all things have an axis that holds them in place. Flor and I were left behind, and that just didn't make sense. First the bird, then Dad, and now what about us? The synchronisation wouldn't stop there. Without Dad, all we could do was fly away or die, like a swarm with no queen bee. This thought, or this realisation, came to me as I watched Flor sitting in the middle of the room, crushing a candle with a fork and concentrating hard, as if her life depended on making that plate of candle mash.

She chopped the candle into small pieces and then squashed them one by one, beginning with the piece nearest the edge of the plate. The wax got stuck between the prongs of the fork. She removed it patiently and started again. Flor is a nexus, I thought. And with nothing to connect, what reason did she have to exist? And what about me? What was the point of me from then on?

She finished destroying the candle and stirred the white powder with her fingers. Then she got up and walked over to where I was sitting.

'Look, I made you thome nithe food,' she said.

Solemnly, she held the plate under my nose. The candle smell caught in my throat. I took the plate, thanked her and pretended to eat, but she went on staring at me. Poor thing, a nexus with no meaning, a string with nothing to tie. I gathered a bit of the powder between my fingers and put it in my mouth. It made me retch, violently. The wax congealed on my tongue, forming a paste I could barely swallow, but Flor didn't take her eyes off me and waited until I'd finished the plate. Then she took it away:

'Very good,' she said. 'You're going to grow big and thtrong.'

I got up and walked around the flat. I didn't want to rinse my mouth and even now I can taste the sour coating of wax on my tongue. When I passed the wardrobe, I looked at the photos. The Sellotape had gone yellow and hard.

'Help me take these down,' I said to Flor. 'We're going on a trip.'

'Are we going to thee the birdies?'

'Yes.'

'Dad too?'

'Yes, all three of us.'

We began carefully unsticking the photos, dropping the bits of tape on the floor and putting the photos in a plastic bag. When night fell, I brought all the remaining candles into my bedroom and lit them; the rest of the flat was plunged into darkness and we almost forgot it was there. We went on taking down the photos, barely making a sound. The candles cast a flickering light and it felt as if the walls were closing in. Flor went over to one of the candles and picked up the saucer. She glanced in my direction because she knew she wasn't supposed to play with them, but I didn't tell her off and that was all the encouragement she needed to hold the flame in front of her face.

'I'm a wiiiiiitch! Mwa-ha-haaaa!' she said, and started doing the laughs Dad had taught her when she was learning the vowels: ha-ha-ha, he-he-he, ho-ho-ho.

The shadows warped her face, her eyes becoming deep caverns and her nose an eagle's beak that stretched across the wall.

'Come here,' I said. 'Now we cut them up like this.'

We broke the photos into tiny bits so it would be impossible to put them back together, then returned them to the bag.

'Now stir.'

She did as she was told, reaching in right to her elbows, then I tied the bag in a double knot. Flor was drowsy, her eyelids were drooping, but she didn't want to go to sleep. She clung to my legs and wouldn't stop asking when we were going to see the birdies.

'Not yet, Flor. First we have to get everything ready. Tomorrow.'

'Tomorrow?'

'Yes, tomorrow, but first you have to sleep.'

I went into the living room and pushed the chest of drawers up against the front door. The chain was already on. I checked the door was double-locked; the peephole was still stuffed with toilet roll. The noise on the stairs had stopped; I suppose by then they were waiting, expectant, in number 302, jostling to press their ears against the wall.

Flor got onto the bed; she could barely keep her eyes open. Those big eyes, thick with eyelashes. What would she do all alone in this world? So defenceless, a pink baby animal with scabs on her head. No one would ever love her, no one would kiss her scabs the way I did.

The clock showed eleven thirty-eight. I covered her with two blankets, put her teddy bear in her arms and gave her a goodnight kiss. Then I said what I always said:

'Sleep tight.'

I think when I lay on top of her she was already asleep. The weight of my body didn't bother her at first. The rest was over in a second. I suppose children don't struggle too much; they think everything's a game. She trembled and kicked her legs a little, but then she gave in to the pressure and fell still, as if she were asleep.

It took me a long time to let go of her. I thought I might not have the strength to move, that I'd be slumped over that little body until they got here. When I finally stood up, I covered her head, unable to look at her. I was scared I might be tempted to touch her and find she was already cold. That's when I decided to remove the blankets from the windows. I left them folded in a pile on the chair, then took Flor in my arms, blanket and all, and carried her into Dad's bedroom.

It's getting light. Everyone who's been out to destroy me all along is sipping champagne and celebrating in Carmen's giant Tent. Deciding, no doubt, the worst ending they can for us. I'm waiting for them calmly, my dry lips pursed to hold in one last laugh. A laugh that will ring out like breaking glass in this cold, completed night. Let them come, let them deliver their verdict. What they don't know is that I've built the only possible victory. What they don't realise is that there's nothing of us left.

CHARCO PRESS

Director & Editor: Carolina Orloff
Director: Samuel McDowell

www.charcopress.com

The Rooftop was published on
90gsm Munken Premium Cream paper.

The text was designed using Bembo 11.5 and ITC Galliard.

Printed in July 2021 by TJ Books
Padstow, Cornwall, PL28 8RW using responsibly
sourced paper and environmentally-friendly adhesive.

MIX
Paper from
responsible sources
FSC® C013056
FSC
www.fsc.org